THE 707 SERIES

RILEY EDWARDS

FREE

A Black Ops Romance

Book 1

The 707 Series

This is a work of fiction. Names, characters, businesses, places, events, and incidents are either the products of the author's imagination or used in a fictitious manner. Any resemblance to actual persons, living or dead, or actual events is purely coincidental.

Cover design: Riley Edwards

Written by: Riley Edwards

Published by: Riley Edwards

Edited by: Elfwerks Editing - https://elfwerksediting.com/

FREE – A Black Ops Romance

First edition – August 2017

This book is dedicated to all the brave men and women who serve or have served in the United States Armed Forces. There are no words to properly convey the sacrifices they make and the appreciation I have for the cost of their service.

A special thanks to the sailors aboard the USS Nimitz (CVN68). I wrote this book while thinking about her crew, especially my daughter who is currently aboard in support of Operation Inherent Resolve.

Godspeed sailors. BRAVO ZULU!

The world lost 31 Heroes 06 Aug 2011. SOC SEAL John W. Faas was among the crew that died that day. Even in death, John continues to inspire all those who knew him and love him. He is not forgotten - never forgotten. His sacrifice and that of his family's reminds us that freedom is never free.

We sleep soundly in our beds because rough men

stand ready in the night to visit violence on those who would do us harm.

Whether it was the writer George Orwell, the essayist Richard Grenier, or the Washington Times columnist Rudyard Kipling who originally wrote those words matters not. The sentiment rings true. We are only afforded the luxuries we have because rough men are willing to stand at the ready. Chief Faas was one of those men.

31 heroes – From a grateful nation.

1

I traced my finger across the cool, smooth headstone over and over. *SHANE McGRATH OWINGS.* It had been five years to the day since I lost my best friend. My only friend.

Growing up the way we did, wealthy and privileged, you didn't have real friends. They were business associates. All of them jockeying for position in the elite Hollywood crowd. Even when we were in high school, especially high school, it was all about who you knew and who your family was. It was never about who you were as a person. No one wanted to know you, they wanted to use you.

The night before Shane left for basic training we went to Santa Monica Pier and sat on the beach for hours talking. When the sun set we laid in the sand, stargazing and telling each other anything and everything we could think of. He knew all my secrets. The only person I could drop the record producer's daughter façade with and be the real Lillian Nelson.

Shane didn't want anything from me. He didn't care that my neighbors were famous rock stars, he didn't care that my house was in an exclusive gated community. Shane's family had more money than mine. In the twisted hierarchy of Hollywood royalty, the Owings' name was higher up the ladder than Nelson.

If anyone found out we had slept on the beach in the sand, we would've been chastised for behaving like low-class Valley kids. Drink a ten-thousand-dollar bottle of scotch and promptly throw it up in your dad's theater room—no problem. Get caught underage drinking at a premier party—brushed under the rug. Get caught sleeping at the beach – end of the world.

Rich kid problems.

The morning Shane left for Army basic training was the day he was free. His family made it clear that if he got on the plane to Georgia, he would no longer be an Owings. Nor would he benefit from all the privilege that name brought, or bought, depending on how you looked at it. When I snuck to Fort

Benning to see his basic training graduation, I was so proud of him. He looked different. Taller, stronger, like he had turned into a real man while there. I missed him every day he was gone. It was the longest twelve weeks of my life. I wrote to him every day, and he wrote me back when he could.

Knowing that Shane had escaped the life he hated made every minute of my loneliness worth it. We spent three awesome days together after graduation before he had to leave for training in Kentucky. We kept in regular contact while he was away, only now, I knew he was keeping secrets. He was evasive when I asked questions about the Army. He tried to cushion the hurt and explained there were things he couldn't tell me about his training or what he would be doing. As much as the distance stung, I understood.

Whenever he called to catch up, it was like nothing had changed. I filled him in on the latest pretentious Hollywood gossip, and he told me what he could about the guys in his unit. I was so jealous. He was living his life and doing what he wanted to do. He spent time in Kentucky, went for training in Texas, and then back to Georgia. Meanwhile, I stayed in California doing everything my father told me to do.

After a while, his calls started coming less and less. And the time it took to return my calls grew longer and longer. Not talking to him every day broke my heart. I missed him so much, but I continued to try and understand he was busy. But it was hard; I was lonely and surrounded by people I despised. Now that Shane was all but gone out of my life, I had no one.

It had been months since I had heard from Shane when he called to tell me he had five days of leave and wanted me to come visit him in Georgia. I was over-the-moon excited and booked my ticket while we were still on the phone. I counted down the days like a prayer; I needed to see him so badly.

When I finally got there, I didn't realize how much I had truly missed him. He was the same, yet so very different. He was rougher now, hardened and more muscular than the last time I saw him almost two years before. He took me around the small town he now lived in and showed me what there was to see. Which wasn't much. But I didn't care; as long as I was with Shane nothing else in the world mattered.

He avoided the base he lived on. Even after I begged him to take me there and show me around, he refused. I never met a single one of the guys in his unit either. When I asked him if he had a girlfriend, he told me he didn't have time for that shit and changed the subject. I was sad there was now so much distance between us. I wanted things to go back to the way they had been when we were in high school.

He asked me a thousand questions about UCLA and what I was studying. He was proud when I told him I had maintained a 3.5 GPA both freshman and sophomore years. I was not a strong student and had pretty much struggled through high school. How did I get into UCLA then? Money. Daddy bought my way in. It never ceased to amaze me what people can buy. You want your average C-student daughter to go to UCLA? No problem. Write a check with a shit ton of zeros for research and an acceptance letter comes in the mail.

My lying, womanizing father always said, "It pays to be rich." I believe the saying actually went "It pays to be a winner", but when you're a rich, egotistical ass, you could say whatever you wanted and people would go along with it.

I spent four wonderful days with Shane.

On the last day, he took me to the Army Infantry Museum and wowed me with all the exhibits. It was so beautiful and humbling there. As I sat in a room full of glass tiles bearing the names of all the Medal of Honor recipients on them, it made me sad to think that for most people the names on the wall were just that - names. A flash on the news or a passing article in the newspaper. Most of us don't think about the sacrifices made by the men and women who served and died for this country. That day, I felt those names deep in my soul. It was a special time that I will carry with me forever.

Shane told me that some days when he needed to think he visited the parade grounds of Soldier Field where he graduated basic. He said it was his favorite place in Georgia. He didn't feel lonely when he was there. He explained how the field was made up of sacred soil taken from all major battlefields his brothers and sisters in arms had fought on. It truly was a beautiful place full of rich history and meaning. I asked him if he felt lonely often and if he regretted his decision to join. He grunted a well-practiced answer about serving his country and never addressed the loneliness part.

Sitting on the grass that afternoon was a wake-up call, or more like a slap in the face actually. I felt my best friend slip away. Shane was not the same person he had been when he left California. Even though he sat only inches from me, I missed my friend. I wanted to scream and cry at the injustice of it. Now, I truly had no one.

When we left the parade grounds, it was like a switch had flipped and he barely spoke to me after that. Short one-word answers and it seemed the excitement of my visit had worn off. I was devastated. By the time the sun was setting, his mood had become even more dark and distant. I tried everything I could think of to get him to open up to me, but he completely shut down. I had watched him do this with his parents, but he'd never closed me out before.

I knew there was something he wasn't telling me. I pleaded with him to talk to me and tell me what was wrong but he refused. That night when we went back to the hotel, instead of ordering room service and watching movies like we'd done every night, he wordlessly grabbed his already packed bag off the bed, threw the strap over his shoulder, and headed toward the door.

I thought we had one more night together before I left the next morning.

But, I didn't.

He stood in front of the door in silence for long moments before he turned and pulled me into him. One minute, I was in his arms kissing him for the very first time, the next he tore me to shreds. I hadn't even recovered from the shock of the kiss we had shared before he told me his news.

He was leaving the next day, too. I was going home to California, and he was leaving on deployment. That was it. No details, no location, no I'll write you. A simple "I'm leaving."

With his hand on the door, he turned to face me, and there was nothing I could do to hide the tears rolling down my cheeks.

I'll never forget his last words to me as long as I live. *We don't say goodbye in the Army, only "I'll see ya' later." I love you. You'll forever be my best friend. I'll see you later, Lily.*

I was stunned into silence. My heart was screaming at me to stop him, talk to him, yell at him. But, my brain wouldn't engage. I was so stupid. And then he was gone. And I didn't even say it back. Something I'll regret for the rest of my life. I never told him that I had always loved him, too.

Thinking back, that's when the lie started. Without Shane around, I had no one. I was surrounded by fake people only pretending to like me. I had no choice but to slip into the role my father demanded I play. That was another lie. I had a choice, I could've done what Shane had done and said *fuck it all* and ran away. Only, I wasn't as strong as him. Especially without him by my side telling me I could be brave.

I tried to fight it at first. But once Shane was gone forever, I gave up. I became exactly what Shane and I had always despised - a fake rich bitch who took her daddy's money. It was pathetic really. If Shane were here, he'd hate who I'd become.

"I miss you, Shane. Not a day goes by I don't think of you." I wiped the tears from my eyes and continued to trace over the smooth letters of his name.

He died two months into his deployment. And in those two months, I wrote countless letters. I poured my heart and soul onto the paper. But the letters remained unsent. They sat in my desk, a constant reminder that Shane was lost to me.

"I wish you were still here. I need you so bad right now. Dad is pushing me to marry Lucas. The prenup has been drawn up. Everyone seems to be happy with it. But I don't love him.

"Remember when we were kids and we told each other what type of person we were going to marry? I don't think *executive producer* was on my list. I don't want this, Shane. I don't want to marry a man because it's good for business. I want someone to love me, the real me. The me I was when I was with you."

I looked around the cemetery and sighed. Damn, I missed Shane. It was a beautiful Southern California day. On a day like today, Shane and I would've taken a drive up the coast to get out of the busy city. No doubt we would've ended up in Monterey, we always did. We both loved to sit on the pier and watch the seals.

Someone setting flowers on a headstone pulled me from my memory, reminding me I wasn't getting ready for a scenic coastal drive with Shane, I'd never have that again. This was all I had left of him - a sad cemetery plot I visited once a year on the anniversary of his death. There were a few people milling about visiting their loved ones. A man sat on a bench not too far from where I was sitting on the grass talking to Shane. His ball cap was pulled low, and his face was buried in his hands obstructing his features. Poor guy looked distraught. I would bet that's what I looked like the first few years I came here. When I was still too afraid to sit on the ground and touch Shane's gravestone.

"You know, I might've mentioned this before, but I really hate your dad. I still cannot believe he had you buried in your family's plot instead of the

National Cemetery. It really burns my ass he refused all military honors at your funeral. What a piece of shit. You deserved that. I miss you so much, but I am damn proud of you. I am proud of your service and your sacrifice."

I pulled in a deep breath. "I love you, Shane, forever. I'll see ya later."

2

"Yo, Lenox, how was leave?" Jasper called out as soon as I walked into the hangar.

"Too short," I answered looking around at the gear stacked in the middle of the large space. "Everyone ready for the load out?"

"Fuck yea. We have a lock on that douche bag Bishop. Time to do some hunting." The wicked smile that lit up his face was almost disturbing.

"Is he still in Turkey?" I asked.

A lot could've changed in the last three days I had been gone.

"Nope. He's in Bulgaria. Remember that Bulgarian hooker, Anna? That horny son of a bitch paid her a visit as soon as he got there. He's been there eighteen hours. We've instructed her to keep slipping him those little blue pills until we can get there," Jasper explained.

"Holy fuck, that's hilarious. What do you think will happen first? He has a heart attack or his dick breaks?" I laughed.

"Don't much care as long as he's there when we get there. We do need to hurry; Anna reported in that she only had ten pills left. The limp dick now requires a double dose to get wood."

"Good thing we're wheels up in five. Lenox, glad you took your sweet ass time getting back. Get your shit sorted?" Clark asked, as the rest of the team joined us in the bay.

Nosy bastard. He loved to poke around in my business. It wasn't a secret what I did when I took leave, but I still didn't want to discuss it.

"Squared up and ready," I answered.

"Load up, boys," Clark yelled.

Today we were catching a ride with the Air Force. The Galaxy C-5 was already on the tarmac loaded up with the cargo it was taking to the Middle East.

"Flyin' first class today, huh, Lenox," Lands, an Airman from the 22nd Airlift Squadron, commented as he walked by me.

He was not wrong. The Galaxy was damn near

first class as far as our normal transports went. This aircraft had the closest thing to commercial seating you could find on a long-haul troop carrier. Depending on who was taking us where, you either had to layer up so you didn't freeze your balls off or you were sweating your ass off and the cargo hold smelled like dirty pits.

"Lands! Long time, brother. I see you added another stripe and a star. Buck Serg, eh? Congratulations," I noted his recent promotion to E-4 Sergeant.

"That's Staff Serg to you, asshole." Lands laughed as he shook my hand. "Have a good flight, she's all ready for you. And be safe over there."

Lands had no idea where we were going or what we were doing. Officially we were headed to Turkey as back up for a Ranger battalion already on the ground. Unofficially we were going to Bulgaria to assassinate an arms dealer who had just made a deal with an even bigger arms dealer from Albania. That deal could not take place. It was our mission to eliminate Bishop before he made it to Albania.

"Copy that. Have a good one," I replied, joining the rest of my team who'd already started boarding.

I looked around Travis' airfield one last time and sucked in a cleansing breath, knowing that it would be my last breath of fresh air for a while. Once we completed this mission, it was a crapshoot if we'd come straight back to the states or if I'd be stuck in the sandbox breathing in dirt and scum for months.

I made my way into the Galaxy and took my seat next to Jasper. He'd given up just as much as I had for his country. We came up through basic, Airborne school, selection, and Ranger school together. He got pulled from selection the same time I did, and once we completed Ranger school we left the regiment and joined the 707.

We were five teams; four men to a team who worked at the 707 research and development unit. Of course, the "research and development" was bullshit. We were twenty men with a highly-specialized skill set. We didn't follow normal Army protocol and chain of command; our orders came directly from the President. We did the dirty work the government could deny.

"Crash code of the day, dirt diver," Clark said and handed each of us a red file folder.

I quickly opened mine and scanned the mission-specific information. This should be a straightforward op; confirm the location of Bishop and call in an airstrike.

"Well fuck me, there will be no fun on this op," Jasper murmured.

"Shut up and enjoy the vacation," I laughed.

I swear most days I thought Jasper had a death wish. He was the first to volunteer for the most dangerous missions, and once he was there, he was balls out. Not reckless, but fearless. He had nothing to lose. His parents were deceased. He was an only child, no wife, and no family. He was the perfect soldier as far as Command was concerned. His need for action and the high that came from it was unparalleled.

"This shit isn't a vacation, it's boring. Man, anyone can confirm a location," he complained.

"Is that so? Confirm the location of a man that the government doesn't want to acknowledge even exists?" I reminded him.

"Yeah, yeah. Still fucking boring."

When the Galaxy jolted forward and began taxiing, I rested my head on the seat and closed my eyes. Reaching into my shirt, I pushed aside the beaded chain of my dog tags and found the smooth links of my necklace. Pulling it out I fingered the silver tree of life pendant, moving it back and forth on the chain. I never traveled without it. It was the only thing I had left of her.

I knew what I was giving up when I joined the 707. I thought I fully understood the ramifications of my decision. What I hadn't planned on was it leaving a hole in my heart so fucking big most days I couldn't catch my breath. I guess Jasper and I were more alike than I cared to admit. I didn't have anything to lose either - I'd already lost it all. I also needed the rush of a mission. The high that came from jumping out of planes and killing bad guys. When the high went away, all I was left with were my thoughts and memories.

Once we were airborne, I tucked the charm back into my shirt and kept my eyes closed. We had a thirteen-hour flight, there would be plenty of time to read the mission brief. I was bone tired and needed to clear my head.

"Do you have eyes on the package?" Clark's voice crackled in my ear.

We had Anna's small house surrounded. Jasper and I peered into her bedroom window to confirm Bishop was still in the house. The rest of the team took up positions as over watch, making sure that we were clear to move around the house freely.

"Affirmative. Eyes on the prize," I answered.

"Christ almighty, his pasty white ass drilling

Anna will forever be burned into my brain," Jasper whispered to me.

"Mission shift, boys. Take him out," Clark advised.

"Please confirm, mission shift?" Jasper asked.

"Take him out," Clark repeated.

A devilish smile tugged the corners of his lips. Fucking A, there was something not right with him.

"The hooker?" I asked.

"Friendly," Clark replied.

I nodded to Jasper, inaudibly telling him to take the lead. He moved us to the side entrance of the house. Thanks to Anna, the door was unlocked allowing us to slip in undeterred. We entered the bedroom where Bishop was still on top of Anna humping her while she lay under him faking her way through what I would suspect was some really bad sex. It sounded like a bad porno set with all the loud ohs and ahs.

Jasper didn't waste any time pulling Bishop off Anna. With one slit to his throat, Bishop lay crumpled on the floor, blood pouring from his wound.

Anna remained on the bed, fully nude, not even so much as flinching when she saw Jasper kill Bishop.

"Took you assholes long enough. Do you know

how many pills I had to give him to keep his dick hard?" Anna's English was impeccable.

"Sorry, sweetheart. We came as quickly as we could," I laughed.

"You're taking him, right? I have another client this evening. I can't have a dead man in my room. It tends to kill the mood. And you'll help clean up the blood," she demanded.

I don't know why but the word *client* made me chuckle. She made it sound like she was a legit executive who was about to have a very important meeting.

"Did he already pay you?" Jasper asked, ignoring her question.

"Not enough. Worst fuck I've had all year. That man doesn't know a woman's pussy from a goat's ass." She got up and walked to Bishop on the floor. "Hurry and wrap him up before more blood gets on the floor."

Anna walked to her closet and pulled out a tarp and a bag full of cut up rags.

"Mission complete," I called in.

"Roger. Five minutes to go," Clark returned.

"Five to go," I relayed to Jasper.

He was already rolling Bishop's body in the tarp. Anna was naked on her knees next to him mopping up the blood with a rag off the worn wood floor.

"What a shame you don't have longer. I can do a lot in five minutes, but I suspect a man like you would need longer than that." She winked at Jasper.

Anna was a beautiful woman. Her deep rich black hair was long and had a slight wave to it, a striking contrast to her pale, smooth skin. What made Anna stand out among all the other Bulgarian women I had met were her eyes. She didn't have the normal dark brown eyes, hers were pale green.

"I don't know, darlin', as hot as you are I might blow my load in two minutes," Jasper flirted back.

"You're smooth. I'm sure you have all the ladies eating out of your hand back home. Too bad you don't need me." Anna tossed another dirty rag on top of Bishop's body. Most of the blood had already been cleaned up.

I checked out the window again keeping watch over Jasper as he readied Bishop for movement.

"We're done here." Jasper rolled Bishop, encasing him in the tarp.

I took one last look out the window. "We're on the move," I radioed Clark.

"Copy that."

"Anna, always a pleasure to see you." I handed her a wad of bills. "Thank you for your time."

"Nice doing business with you. Be well," she replied, taking the money and leaving the room, not bothering to cover her naked body.

Jasper and I carried Bishop out the front door where a beat-up cargo van met us on the small street. It would be a bloody miracle if this rust bucket could make it to the extraction point. We tossed Bishop in the back and jumped in, pulling the rear door closed behind us.

"I swear if that woman wasn't a hooker I would take her home and marry her," Jasper joked.

"She is hot. You know I think she gives 707 members a discount. You should hit her up," Levi spoke as he maneuvered his way around the potholes in the bumpy dirt road.

"I wouldn't fuck that woman with your dick, which is unfortunate because she is sexy as hell," Jasper chuckled.

"Good job, boys. We're gonna drop this scum bag off in Izmir and hit Kosovo. We have new intel on Roman."

Shit, this was going to be a long trip. Roman was another arms dealer, only he specialized in surface-to-air missiles. We'd been on the hunt for him for the better part of two years. He needed to be taken out. The worst part about Roman was he was an American. A special forces soldier trained by the 707. A few years ago, he went off the rails and went AWOL. Roman had vanished into thin air. He resurfaced a year later as an information broker. It didn't take long for him to raise enough capital to start selling weapons.

We had to outsmart him because we couldn't out maneuver him. Roman was one of us, he knew our tactics. His betrayal was felt deep around Command. When one of your own turns on you, it made you question everything you thought you knew.

3

I found comfort in the familiarity of the weathered stone beneath my fingertips. After all these years, even in death, Shane was the only constant in my life. The only person who I felt like the real me around.

"Ten years. It's hard to believe you've been gone ten years. Sometimes it feels like just yesterday we were hanging out, eating pizza, and complaining about what our families expected of us. But other times it feels like a lifetime ago."

I angrily wiped my tears away. I wondered if this day would ever get easier. Would the pain ever lessen? Each and every day over the last ten years, I had regretted never telling Shane my true feelings for him. I was always afraid that if I told him I was in love with him, I would lose the only friend I ever had.

I was so stupid. Maybe if I had admitted my feelings things would've been different. Maybe we could've run off together and lived a normal life away from our screwed-up families.

"I wish I would've told you how much I loved you. I wish I had been brave enough back then to take the leap and tell you that it was always you, that there would never be another man for me. I was such a coward."

Now look at me, I was thirty years old and the proud owner of divorce papers. The ink was still wet when Lucas told me that he was buying me out of the house because Stella, his new girlfriend, wanted to live in it.

Fuck him, and fuck the house. It didn't take long after we were married for Lucas to start cheating on me. He screwed every wannabe starlet that walked into his office. His lame excuse was he had to take other women because I refused to make him a father. How that made any sense whatsoever was beyond me. But there was a stark difference in him after he found out I had an IUD inserted to prevent pregnancy. He refused to use condoms, and I refused to get pregnant.

After I caught him screwing the star of his latest TV show, I refused to have sex with him at all. That was one month into our marriage. I spent four long years married to a man who disrespected me every day.

To make matters worse, my dad knew. Hell, my dad saw my husband pick up women from events they attended together. He completely condoned Lucas' behavior, even went as far as telling me that was what men did when they were lonely and not being taken care of by their wives. Thank God my father never remarried after my mother died. He just tramped around Hollywood taking a new piece of ass whenever he wanted.

"I bought a new townhouse in Malibu. It is right off PCH. It's perfect, Shane, you would love it. I have a great view of the beach, and from my balcony, I can see Pepperdine. I left Lucas with all the God-awful highfalutin furniture he'd insisted on and went to Pottery Barn and furnished my new place. I finally have something that is mine."

I had only been out of my old house in Hidden Hills for a month, but I was already feeling worlds better than I did when I lived in that lonely mansion. Lucas was all about showing off what we had. Pompous prick. He was pissed I would never give him access to my trust fund. My father had told him that there was fifty million dollars in my trust and urged Lucas to have me invest that money in their new studio. I refused.

I refused for many reasons, but largely because there was no longer fifty million sitting in a trust fund. Almost all of it was gone.

A few years back, I had an epiphany sitting here talking to Shane. I took stock in my life and found I came up lacking. I had truly turned into a worthless rich brat. I was so ashamed of who I had become I decided to change my life. I wanted to be someone that Shane would be proud of.

I took my trust fund money and used it for something good. Something I was proud of. I co-founded the McGrath Carter Center. Shane was my co-founder. After all, it was his idea. One night after we snuck out of some movie premiere after party, Shane was talking about how wasteful Hollywood was. All the parties, all the expensive dresses, the food that goes to waste.

He was right. It was a disgrace to be so damn wasteful when there were so many people in our local communities who were struggling or had nothing. We talked in-depth about how much better this world would be if people would work together, helping each other. That if Hollywood execs would get their heads out of their asses and donate all the leftover food to homeless shelters it wouldn't go into the trash.

"We opened another center in Reseda. The location is perfect, right next to a bus stop. We got a sizable donation a few months back that allowed us to add a dedicated library and after-school program. The homework room is awesome. And the gym is a kid's paradise. I remember what you told me about people being the happiest when they feel useful and like they are making a difference. We implemented that, too. There is no charge to use the center, but you must volunteer.

The local Big Brothers Club volunteered to do all of the outside clean-up and maintenance. Shane, the center is fully staffed by all volunteers. Even the director I hired has her own family there cleaning and tutoring every day she works. I think I have found the family I was always looking for. I just wish you were here to see it."

I looked around the cemetery. Not much had changed over the last ten years. The trees surrounding the area had grown larger, a few more shrubs and flower beds had been added, but for the most part, it was oddly reassuring that it remained the same.

After so many years of coming to the same place, you start to recognize the people who come to visit their loved ones on the same day you do. It's like we shared some weird cosmic connection; the people we loved were taken from this earth on the same day. This was the first year that I had not seen Mr. Vasquez since I had started coming. With a quick check to my left, I saw that there was a new headstone next to his wife's. He died almost a year ago. I am sure he's happy to be with his beloved wife. He missed her dearly and would tell me stories about her as we sat in the grass together.

I glanced to my right and saw a man I had seen many times before. He now had a full beard covering his face, but the same ball cap pulled low and same black dirty work boots. I didn't see him every year I came, but I saw him a lot. I checked the headstone he sat in front of, and it was a woman's name. The date on the stone placed her to be around what could be his mother's age. That was purely a guess, I had never actually seen his face to gauge his age. He was always gone when I was leaving.

"Oh, I forgot to tell you, we expanded on the food pick up. We now have contracts with all major studios to donate any leftover food. That includes parties and craft services from casting, as well. I am so proud of that contract. Do you know how many families we feed nightly with that food? It is distributed to three centers. I hope by next year I'll have another center to tell you about. Rebecca was talking to me about possibly expanding out of state. That is really expensive, though. I don't want to do anything that will jeopardize what we have here. Maybe in a few years when my trust fund makes some more money. I keep ten million in there to invest. The centers are fully funded for now.

"And besides, cheating douchenozzle broke our prenup by fucking all of Hollywood and not being careful about it. He now owes me a mint. I didn't want to accept the settlement. Only now I am, I want his money put to good use."

I was so happy I let my lawyer talk me into enforcing the deal of our prenup. My lawyers told me I deserved Lucas' money for all the years of pain and suffering. I didn't believe that to be true; I could've left anytime I wanted. I stayed out of some dumb sense of obligation to my father not to tarnish the Nelson name with a divorce, which was laughable because everyone knew what a lying bastard he was.

But what I would do was take Lucas' money and give it to my centers. He never donated to anything in his life, stingy prick. But he would now, to the tune of one hundred million dollars. That is what he paid for all the ass he screwed over the years. When I brought that to his attention, he laughed in my face and told me it was money well spent. Asshole.

"I love you, Shane. I'll see ya later."

I stood up and started to brush the grass off my pants, and I caught a glimpse of the man in the ball cap wiping his eyes before he hurried off.

I gave Shane one last look. "I miss you so much."

4

"Lenox, watch your two o'clock. Direction of movement is east," Jasper called over from his cover behind a stack of wooden shipping containers.

"Copy that." I slowed my breathing, my heart rate coming under control.

My cheek was a mere cunt hair away from my black polymer .308 stock, and I had a perfect line of sight down the Leupold Mark4 scope. All I needed to do was wait for this asshole to show himself again.

Silcox had barricaded himself in a room with hostages. We wanted to take him alive to get intel on Roman, but now he'd left us no choice but to eliminate him.

We lost Roman five years ago, and he had only now resurfaced. Silcox was one of his pilots, we'd hoped to bring him in peacefully. Unless he gave himself up, that looked to be a non-option.

When I saw the red hair come into my crosshairs, I blew out a slow breath and pulled the trigger.

"He's down," Jasper announced.

"I'm going in," Clark informed the team.

I kept my .308 dialed in on the building Clark was entering, making sure he had cover as he ran across the street. Even after he ducked into the building, we all continued to watch the street, not taking any chances that this was a setup.

"Clear," came through the com in my ear. "Room is empty. Not even a desk. Fucking empty. Hostages scattering."

I watched as five women ran out of the building, two holding infants.

"Goddamn pussy, hiding behind women and children," I muttered.

"Another dead end. Where the fuck is this asshole?"

"Extraction one, we're ready for pick up," Clark called into Command.

"Roger that. Extraction one."

"At least the Adriatic Sea is nice this time of year. We could be sitting in Afghanistan sweating our balls off," Jasper said as he shoveled in another bite of his grilled lobster.

He was not wrong. Of all the places our search for Roman had led us, Vis, a small Croatian island, was the nicest. In another life, I could've imagined vacationing here. The southern beaches were crystal clear, beautiful rock formations made hidden coves, where vacationers could bask in the warm sun.

She would've loved it here. The quaint local shops were right up her alley. I could picture her walking up and down the streets, tugging me behind her as she excitedly poked around the stores.

Another life.

That was a long time ago, and those thoughts were dangerous. However, I couldn't stop the what ifs. What if I hadn't been so afraid? What if I had asked her to come with me. What if I had said no when I was approached by Command. Would we have been together? Had a family by now?

Any thoughts of having a wife, or a family, were gone. I made that decision when I said yes. Family had no place in Command. Family was a weakness, something that could and would be used against you.

I made my choice, and there was nothing I could do about it now.

"And the women are spectacular," Clark added as a barely dressed woman walked by. "We have a few hours, boys. Feel free to play, as long as you are ready for wheels up at thirteen hundred tomorrow. Enjoy your R&R. God knows I will."

Without waiting for us to answer, Clark got up to follow the young woman in the bathing suit.

"Shit, Clark has the right idea. I need to get laid. You up to hit that bar we passed by the hotel?"

I thought back over the last twelve years and tried to remember all the women I had slept with. Hundreds. There was a time, in the beginning, I fucked any and every woman who looked my way. And it was not hard to pick up women. With all of the training we did, each of us had the body of a fitness model. Only our muscle was a necessity, not vanity.

Anything to forget her. Anything to forget the burning regret in my gut. I thought I had fucked her out of my system, but then I saw her again. And everything I thought I had worked out came rushing back.

There I was again nailing a different woman in every city we visited across the world. Some days it was because of all the built-up frustration and adrenaline, and I needed a release. Other times I found women who resembled her so I could pretend like some sick fuck I was with her.

When did this merry-go-round end? I needed to be done once and for all. I had to let the memory of her go. I just didn't know how.

"Yeah sure. I'll get a drink with you," I answered.

Jasper stood and fished out his wallet, throwing a hundred-dollar bill on the table. Much more than was needed. When the beautiful waitress first came over to take our order, Jasper immediately started flirting with her. When she turned him down on his offer for drinks later, she explained it was because she was a single mother living with her parents.

"That will make her day," I said nodding toward the bill.

"I don't know what you're talking about. You ready to go on a pussy hunt?" Typical Jasper saying the crassest thing he could think of to cover up an act of generosity.

Idiot.

"There is something wrong with you. You know that, right?" I laughed.

"That's what your mama said the last time she kicked me outta bed," he fired back.

"That's funny. Because my mama tended to like younger boys. You must be even more fucked up than I thought if that hoe bag kicked you outta her bed."

And that was the truth. Jasper knew very little about my old life. When we were coming up through selection, I gave him the cliff notes version but never got into the details of my fucked-up family. Jasper knew bits and pieces about *her*. He didn't know her name, no one did. I never allowed myself to say her name out loud. She was just a memory now. One I needed to forget.

"That's fucked, bro. Was your Ma really like that?"

"Yep. She fucked every friend I had in high school. My dad knew too, and couldn't have cared less. While she was fucking every young male in a fifty-mile radius, my dad was fucking every model who would let him. He was so screwed up, sometimes I would come home from school, and there would be topless models he had just finished with still by the pool. You know what that asshole would do?" I didn't bother waiting for him to answer. "He would ask me if I wanted a piece, too."

The fire burned in my gut at the memory. And that is why I had to leave. Why I joined the Army. I could not take my parents' dysfunction and downright disgusting morals.

"Man, your parents sound jacked."

"More than you know."

The walk to the bar was done in silence, each of us scanning the streets and the street vendors as we passed. A hazard of the job; you could never let your guard down.

The bar was packed even in the early after dinner hour. Tourists and locals alike drank together and danced around a small dance floor.

"What can I get you?" an older woman asked in English.

"That obvious, huh?" I asked. "Any dark beer in a bottle."

"Just a lucky guess." She winked at me. "And for you?" She turned to Jasper.

"The same," he replied.

Jasper and I both only ever ordered bottled beer while in foreign countries. I didn't need any chance of getting Montezuma's revenge and shitting my brains out from some weird bacteria. I wouldn't even chance it by drinking anything that had ice in it.

"Here you boys are. Enjoy." The bartender slid two bottles of Guinness our way.

"'Preciate it."

Just as I was about to ask Jasper his thoughts on Roman, two beautiful blondes sat beside us.

"Well, hey there handsome," the first blonde purred. "You gotta name?"

It was hard holding back my laugh - picking up women was easier than shooting fish in a barrel. What women like these two didn't understand is men liked the thrill of the chase, we liked to hunt and conquer.

Luckily for them, we were on short time and didn't have time for the hunt.

"My name is Tom, this here is Brian," Jasper replied with a fake Texas twang.

"Ohh Sarah, listen to that accent. I'm Stephanie, and this is my sister Sarah. We're Americans, too. We're from Vermont." The older of the two made the introduction. "Well, cowboy Tom, do you wanna go dance? Leave these two here to get to know each other."

Jasper winked at me and took Sarah's outstretched hand. "Don't mind if I do, ma'am."

Jasper, now in full character of cowboy Tom, pulled Sarah to the dance floor and swayed to the music.

"So, Brian, what do you guys do in Texas?" Stephanie asked. Her voice was soft and nervous.

"Garbage disposal," I replied.

When you're making up a lie as a cover, it's best to stick to as much of the truth as you could. And the truth was I was in the garbage disposal business, just not the garbage she was thinking of.

"That sounds..." she trailed off.

"Boring. I know. Let's talk about you. What brings you and your sister to beautiful Vis?"

Stephanie blew out a breath before she answered, "That's boring too. I caught my fiancé with another woman. My sister thought it would be a good idea to take a vacation and find someone to... you know..."

"Ah. Yes, revenge sex. How's that working out for you?" I asked.

This woman didn't look like she had an aggressive bone in her body. Not like her sister. She would need someone to woo her and coax her into bed. Now, by the looks of what Sarah was doing to Jasper on the dance floor, they'd be gone within the next ten minutes, disappearing into a closet or bathroom for a quickie.

"We leave tomorrow, and there has been no revenge sex." Stephanie lowered her gaze to the table. "I'm not the type of woman that a man wants to take home and have sex with."

"You are right about that. But, wrong about the reasons why. Look at me." I stopped and waited for her to bring her eyes to mine. "You are a beautiful woman. But you have a way about you that is gentle and timid. For a man that can be intimidating. Let's just say you don't put off the one-night stand vibe."

"What vibe do I give off?" she asked.

"The long-term relationship vibe."

"Oh, God. I just wanted to come here and have sex. Now you're telling me I've been doing it all wrong. I want to get laid. Is that too much to ask? Sheesh."

I tossed my head back and laughed.

"No, Stephanie, it's not. Let's go." I stood up and reached my hand down.

Stephanie looked at my hand, then looked at me. "Really?" She smiled.

"Come, sweetheart. I'll fuck you so long and well, you'll forget that lying cheating asshole's name."

She grabbed my hand, and I led her through the throng of dancing bodies until we found Sarah and Jasper. They were all but fucking on the dance floor.

"We're outta here. Sarah, I am in room 201 if you need your sister," I yelled over the music.

"She won't. Sarah will be all tied up. She asked

me to show her some of my rodeo skills. See you in the morning," Jasper replied.

The women did some strange womanly wave thing with their fingers, and I led Stephanie out of the bar.

By the time we made it to my hotel room, I wondered if she had changed her mind.

"You sure you want this? Revenge sex isn't all it's cracked up to be. I don't want you to wake up tomorrow and regret anything."

"Have you ever had revenge sex?" she asked.

"No, not revenge sex. But I've been using sex as a way to get over someone for the last twelve years," I answered her honestly.

"Has it worked?" she whispered.

"Yes, for a few hours. But after that, the guilt hits and you wonder if it was worth it."

"I just want to forget for a few hours. Can we forget together? I'll worry about the guilt later." She tried to smile, but it didn't reach her eyes. This woman was going to regret this in the morning. "Please. I need to forget what I saw. I need to feel something other than his betrayal," she begged.

Call it a good deed, call it me being a weak douche bag who needed the same thing - I just wanted to forget her for a few hours and get lost in someone else's body. I would deal with the shame and regret later.

I unlocked the door to the hotel and quickly ushered her in. Before the door fully shut, I had Stephanie in my arms. My lips found hers and my body went on autopilot. No feeling, no emotion. Just numb.

5

Twelve years.

How the years had flown by. I was busier than ever with McGrath Carter. My centers were the perfect distraction from the nonsense that was my personal life. Once my father found out my part in the centers, he all but disowned me. He said the centers were fine to fund, but the thought of me actually working in them was insulting to the Nelson name and low class. He thought waving that threat in front of me would deter me from my goals. Little did he know, that was all the push I needed to keep going when things got difficult.

I was finally free of the Nelson curse.

"Hey, Shane. I wish you were here to see what we've done with the centers. We have ten up and running. I think they are exactly what you'd envisioned. People helping people. These centers have brought me so much joy. Do you know the last time I wore a designer suit or carried some lame ten-thousand-dollar handbag? Forever ago, that's when. I am free to be me. I really wished you could've been there when I told my father to kiss my ass. I thought he'd stroke out right then and there."

I stopped speaking and bit my lip. Damn, that last statement might've been insensitive.

"I went to your father's funeral. I know that it is in bad taste to speak ill of the dead so I will refrain. It was a nice funeral. Your mother pulled out all the stops and made sure your father's send-off was as gaudy and extravagant as humanly possible. I didn't go back to the house for the party she was having. I hope that's okay. I thought you'd be alright with me paying my respects graveside."

I brushed my hand over his name. The headstone needed to be polished. I would have to remember to have someone come out and clean it. Or now that his father was dead, I wondered if I could petition to have his body moved to the National Cemetery where he could be honored as the hero he was.

I raised my face toward the sun and soaked in

some of its warmth. It was a busy day at the cemetery. People were milling about, some laying flowers and quickly leaving, and others like me sitting in the grass talking to their loved ones.

The man in the ball cap was sitting, staring at the gravestone in front of him. So many times I wanted to go over and ask him if he was alright, but I always thought better of intruding on his personal time. I wouldn't appreciate someone trying to talk to me while I was spending time with Shane.

"Remember Rebecca? I know I've told you about her. She is my right-hand woman. Her eldest son just started driving and is now volunteering three nights a week as a tutor for the middle school kids. We had some issues with a few rough kids coming in and trying to cause trouble. But the community as a whole put a stop to that immediately. It actually made the LA Times. Shop owners from up and down the block came to stand in front of the center, not letting the rough kids enter. Rebecca's husband and son came out and talked with the boys and invited them in. We showed them the rock wall, basketball courts, and asked them if they would come in a few nights a week to teach the smaller kids how to play ball. They've been a fixture ever since."

I tried my hardest not to cry anymore when I

came to visit, but I couldn't help it. Twelve shitty years later and it still hurt. Year after year I sat and talked to Shane like he could hear me. Like he was still alive and cared about what I was doing with my life. How many more years could I come and stare at his name carved into an ugly white piece of granite? God, I hated Shane's family. White granite for a headstone. Did they not know him at all? He would take a sledgehammer to this ugly thing if he were here.

But Shane would never see it. He'd never hear my words. He'd never love me the way I still love him every day. I've tried to move on. I had been fucking married. I've had boyfriends. I've slept with men. But they were always lacking. No one is Shane. No one made me feel like he did. We shared one kiss, and it was better than any other kiss I ever had. I think I hated him a little for that. His soft lips touching mine and the tangling of our tongues bound me to him forever. Even in death, I was still tied to him.

I worked as much as humanly possible, anything to keep my mind busy. I was thirty-two and lonely.

I put my face in my hands and sobbed.

"I fucking miss you, Shane. I am still lost without you. I don't know how I will ever get over you. But I hope I do. I hope that one day I'll be able to move on. I am so lonely."

"Excuse me, Miss?" I heard from behind me.

Oh no. I didn't realize how loud I'd been while I was crying. I hoped I hadn't disturbed anyone else.

"I'm sorry," I mumbled.

"Lillian Nelson?" the man asked.

I lifted my head out of my hands and looked over my shoulder. Two men stood behind me both wearing black suits. All the fine hairs on the back of my neck started to tingle. Something wasn't right.

"Yes, I'm Lillian Nelson. May I help you?" I quickly stood up and faced the men.

"Sorry to disturb you, ma'am. There's been an accident, and we need you to come with us," the second man spoke.

"I'm sorry, who are you?" I asked.

I looked around, and the cemetery seemed to have cleared out. The man with the ball cap had gone, and the nearest couple was at least a hundred yards away. Unease hit my belly. Something was definitely wrong. I patted my back pocket checking for my cell phone. I normally didn't bring it out of the car when I came to visit Shane. This was my special time with him, I didn't want interruptions.

Thank God, this one time, I brought it with me. I felt marginally better knowing I could call for help.

"Sorry, I am Detective Michaels, and this is Detective Nicolson," Detective Michaels made the introduction.

"Detective? May I ask what sort of accident there could be that would send two detectives out to a cemetery to find me?" Nothing was making sense.

"We'll explain everything once we're in the car, ma'am," Detective Nicolson spoke up.

"If you don't mind, I'd like to see your badges, please. And, I have my car here. I'm happy to drive myself."

Detective Michaels reached into the inside of his suit jacket giving me a clear view of the weapon on his hip.

"Ma'am, I think it's best if you just come with us, we'll explain in the car." The tone of his voice had changed; it was clearly laced with impatience.

"No, that's quite alright. I will follow you to the station." I was trying to think of some way to get away from these men without causing a scene. What if I was wrong and they were just two nice police officers. God knows that my imagination could get the best of me.

"What is this about?" I asked again, noting that neither man had produced a badge.

Both men quickly stepped toward me. Detective Michaels had his weapon drawn, and Nicolson was reaching for me. I stepped back dodging his touch and lost my footing. I stumbled backward and fell to the ground landing next to Shane's headstone. Before I could get my bearings, something wet hit me in the face.

The scream started in my belly and traveled up, building in my lungs, before it exploded out of my mouth. I scrambled back from the crumpled bodies on the ground. Blood was oozing out of both of their heads. I didn't understand how it happened. I didn't hear a gunshot, I didn't see anyone near us. This couldn't be happening.

No, no, no! I continued to scream and closed my eyes, I rolled to my knees to get up and run. As soon as I was on my feet, strong arms wrapped around my middle from behind and I was pulled tight against a wall of hard body.

"Quiet Lily," a man whispered. "Come on, you have to get out of here," the man spoke again, his lips a hair's breath away from my ear, and his scratchy beard tickled the side of my neck.

I tried to push away to run, but he was too strong.

His grip was ungiving no matter how hard I tried I couldn't move.

"Lily! Calm down, we need to go now," he said. This time there was a deadly urgency in his tone.

I belatedly remembered that voice and stopped struggling. Truth be told, I stopped breathing altogether. It was impossible. My mind had to be playing tricks on me.

His hold loosened and I was able to turn in his arms. I could barely see his face because a ball cap was pulled low on his brow and he had a full, thick beard. But those eyes. I would know those eyes anywhere.

"Shane?"

6

My name fell from her lips like a litany and my body locked. I hadn't been called that name in twelve years. Out of the corner of my eye, I saw the glint of light reflecting off a scope reminding me we weren't out of danger yet. And I wasn't Shane Owings anymore. I didn't have the luxury of a lover's reunion. I was Carter Lenox, special operator for the 707.

"We need to move. Now." I pulled her hand and started to run, giving her no chance to argue.

She struggled to keep up with my rigorous pace as I weaved in and out of the headstones and memorial benches. I had no idea how many men had been sent to take me out or how many were now on their way.

We got to my rental car, and I shoved Lily in through the driver side door. She scrambled over the center console before she landed in the passenger seat.

No sooner were the keys in the ignition when the first shot hit the back windshield and blew it out.

"Get down. All the way to the floor board," I instructed.

I didn't wait for her to comply before I threw the Mustang in gear and gunned the engine. I regretted not renting a faster car, but I thought this was going to be a nice little trip for some R&R. How fucking wrong I was.

I was almost to the exit of Forrest Lawn, and I looked right and left gauging the traffic. Right would've been the smart way to turn, but the railroad and zoo were that way. Too many damn kids would be out in the open. Left it was, smack dab into the Warner Brother's studio traffic. Fuck I was driving a bright red Mustang. It wasn't like I could blend into the traffic.

I hoped that I had one small advantage; I knew these roads like the back of my hand. We were playing this game on my home turf. Two cars followed close behind, and more shots rang out, all missing the car as I continued to swerve through the thick traffic.

"Who are you?" Lily asked.

Once we were past the studio traffic, I accelerated again and made another left. If I could just make it over the Cahuenga Pass, I could lose them in the Hollywood Hills. There was a small access road that led to the Hollywood reservoir. Only locals knew where the entrance was, and if I timed this just right, I could exit the pass and they'd blow right past me.

"Who are you?" Lily asked again.

I veered in and out of traffic like I was playing some fucked-up game of Grand Turismo. The exit for the reservoir was coming up on the right. I stayed in the far-left lane until the very last second. I slammed on the brakes, swerving across three lanes of traffic to make the exit. Both cars blew by us at a high rate of speed, unable to cross over the lanes in time to follow me.

I hit the overpass that led to the reservoir and slowed. A new housing track had been built overlooking the water. I drove through the neighborhood to make sure that no other cars were following us before I turned down the access road. I drove past the dam to the uppermost part of the reservoir and found the small dirt road we used to go to and park when we were kids.

I stopped the car and looked down at Lily. She was still balled up on the floorboard of the car, staring at me as if she'd seen a ghost. I guess in this case she had. I was supposed to be dead.

She was even more beautiful than when we were younger. She was hot when we were teenagers. The guys at school used to fall over themselves to get to her. The fact that she turned them all down just made them try harder. She was all Southern California girl, the typical stereotype you'd see in a movie. But when you got close to her you realized there was nothing typical about this girl.

Even a disheveled mess, my body reacted. Her long blonde hair was piled on top of her head, fashioned in some sort of messy stylish bun. Beautiful sun-kissed tanned skin that called to me. I had seen her over the years, but never this close. I never allowed myself to really look at her. I knew if I got close, and saw her amber eyes, I would break down and tell her who I was.

I was a fucking fool.

Why hadn't I told her how I felt before I left for basic? Why hadn't I kissed her in high school? Why hadn't I been the one to take her innocence? I could have. I saw the way she looked at me when she thought I wasn't looking. But I was a dumbass and was too afraid I'd screw it up. It wasn't worth losing her friendship. My parental role models sucked. What if I turned into my dad and became a cheating bastard? I would've hated myself if I hurt her that way.

"Who are..."

"You know who I am, Lily," I cut her off.

"What? How? I don't understand. I don't know who you are," she stammered.

"You can get up now. We lost them."

"Lost who? What's going on?"

I closed my eyes and pushed my head back against the head rest. I didn't know how to begin this conversation. As much as I missed her and wished that I had made different choices, I never once imagined that I would ever speak to her again. This moment that was happening was an impossibility. She was never supposed to see me again.

"Shane. Please, I'm scared. I don't understand any of this." Her tears gutted me. They always did. Every year when she sat beside an empty grave and talked to me as if I was buried there with tears pouring down her cheeks, it killed me.

Yet, every year I forced myself to go.

"Those two men at the cemetery were bad guys," I started.

"I don't care about any of that," she screamed. "I buried you. I was there when you were lowered into the ground. I was there after the hole was...was... filled in. I watched the whole time. I don't understand how you're here."

"Lily. I can't explain."

"You better find a way Shane, or I swear to God I will jump out of this car and run away."

I couldn't help the smile that formed, it happened of its own accord. Just hearing the spunk in her voice transported me back to the days when everything was easy and carefree. She and I spending lazy Sundays hiking these trails.

"Remember when I convinced you to go skinny dipping? And we didn't realize we were so close to the bike path and that family rode by. You ducked under the water and tried to hold your breath until they passed. Only you couldn't do it, and you popped out of the water. The dad caught a look at your boobs and fell off his bike."

I chuckled, but my little reminder of our past together seemed to only upset her more.

"Why? Why did you leave me? Why would you pretend to be dead all these years? Twelve fucking years, Shane. I have cried and mourned you for twelve years," she sobbed. I tried to pull her closer to me, but she recoiled. "Don't you dare touch me."

That fucking hurt. She'd never pulled away from me. I had always been the one she ran to for comfort. I blew out a breath and readied myself to tell her the truth, or at least part of it.

"Remember when I was in Texas for training?" I asked.

"Yeah."

"After I passed Airborne school, I was recruited by a special unit - the 707 Research and Development group. Upon completion of Ranger school, I was sent to my new unit."

"What does that have to do with you pretending to be dead?"

"The team I am on is...unique. My death was faked, and all traces of my old life were scrubbed clean. It was safer for everyone involved."

"Safer? I don't understand. We all thought you were dead, Shane. Do you understand what you did to all of us?"

"Yes," I exploded as shame washed over me. "I know what I did. I was there. I watched my own fucking funeral and had to be held back by my team leader not to go to you."

"You were there?"

"I sat in the back and watched. I watched my prick of a father stand tall and proud and talk about my military accomplishments as if he gave a fuck. I watched my bitch of a mother take comfort in some young guy my age. And I watched you. The only person at that whole farce who actually knew me and gave a damn that my life had ended. I watched the woman I love break down. And not only could I not comfort her, but I also caused it. And, I did it on purpose."

Ah fuck.

"Where have you been?" she asked.

"Everywhere. All over the world."

"Was that you in the cemetery? I mean, sitting on the bench."

This was going to hurt her more than me faking my death. This is what made me a selfish prick.

"Yes. I was there every year."

"Oh my God. Why would you do that? How could you sit twenty feet from me and not tell me? You know I would've kept your secret. I would've never told." She was back to crying uncontrollably.

I slid the seat back as far as it would go and pulled Lily over and into my lap. She could protest all she wanted, but she would do it with me hugging her. Once I had her settled in, I wrapped my arms around her and held her tight. I was home. After all these years, I could finally breathe.

"I'm so sorry. I knew it was wrong and selfish. But I had to do it. For 364 days of the year my heart ached, and for one day I could feel again. I have traveled the globe and seen things that you couldn't begin to imagine, but for a few hours one day a year I got to sit in the light and listen to you talk. It was the only thing that kept me going, knowing that if I survived another year I could come home to you. For as long as you stayed, I could soak up some of your love and goodness."

Her eyes lifted to mine, and she stroked my bearded cheek with her small hand. I leaned into her touch, marveling in how soft her skin was when suddenly her touch was gone. A millisecond later, a resounding slap rang out in the car accompanied by the stinging sensation on my face. Her hand pulled back again, but before she could slap me again, I caught it.

"I deserved that, Lily, but don't hit me again. You wanna scream at me? Fine, I know I fucked up. But I swear to you, it was for your protection."

"You keep saying that, Shane, but I don't get how

me thinking you were dead was for my protection," she screamed.

Jesus Christ my ears were ringing.

"Because you are the one and only thing that can be used against me. If someone took you, they could use you to get to me. Or if I was captured and someone showed you a picture of me chained up and beaten, you'd turn yourself over to them to save me. I couldn't take any chances with you. If I was dead and all traces of Shane Owings were wiped clean, you would be safe. No one would know about you."

"Who is someone? You're in the Army, lots of soldiers have wives and families," she protested.

"I'm not in the fucking regular Army. I am not in a research and development brigade; I belong to a black ops unit. I track down and eliminate the worst of the worst criminals around the world. The very people our government has to deny exist, they send me to kill.

"Kill?" Lily whispered.

"Yes, Lillian. I am a government-trained killer. That is where I've been the past twelve years. Killing people."

7

I watched as Shane's eyes changed. It happened quickly, but I saw it. One second he was my Shane, his green eyes soft and gentle. The next his eyes turned cold and shut off. I watched him do this in Georgia all those years ago too. Only now he had perfected it.

I hate to admit that I was scared for a moment until I remembered that this was my Shane; he would never hurt me.

I couldn't believe he was really there in the car sitting with me. My mind was reeling. I had a thousand questions swirling in my head. I desperately wanted answers, but the overwhelming relief I felt won out.

"I missed you," I admitted.

"You wouldn't have if you'd known what I had turned into." Even his voice had a hard edge now.

"I know now who you've turned into, and I still missed you."

I reached for his face, and he caught my hand again. We locked eyes for long moments before he released my hand. There was a silent trust, him letting go of my hand. I had forgotten that there were many times we had both witnessed his mother slapping his father while she called him all sorts of filthy names.

"I'm sorry. I forgot." I didn't need to explain any further - he understood.

He didn't answer me, he just leaned into my touch. I gently rubbed the hair on his face with my thumb. I couldn't take my eyes off of him. I was afraid this was all going to be a dream. And if it was, I needed a few more minutes of touching him and hearing his voice. In my dreams, I never heard his voice.

He had changed so much over the last twelve years. The last time I saw him, he was twenty - still a boy. Now he was all man. Broader and bigger. Time had been kind to him. He was even hotter now, if that were possible. He had his dad's movie star good looks, dark hair and complexion, but his mother's green eyes. There was a reason his mother screwed men half her age; because she could. She was that stunning.

It felt so good to be in his arms. "I really missed you," I whispered. "And as weirded out and angry as I am, I can't stop looking at you. I am so happy to have you back." His eyes came open and looked at me.

"Lily, I am not back. Now that this cover is blown I will ditch this alias and get a new one."

"You're not leaving me. You can't. I won't let you. And what about me? They know about me now."

"Which means you'll have to relocate as well," he replied.

"No. I'm not leaving my centers."

Was he crazy? Well, that was a given; he did fake his own death, which I believe might be the definition of crazy.

"Would you rather them be bombed and innocent children killed? Besides, Rebecca can oversee them. And you have center managers in each location now too," he answered.

"Come again? How do you even know all of that?" I asked.

"You told me most of it. The rest I looked into."

I told him? Of course, I did. Every year I updated

him on every part of my life. I spent hours sitting at his grave telling him every personal thing about my life.

"Look at me, Lily." I brought my eyes back to his. "I am so proud of you - the woman you have become, all that you overcame, and all that you have accomplished. You took some crazy ramblings from a sixteen-year-old boy and turned it into something that's great. And I really wished I could've seen the look on your father's face when you told him to finally kiss your ass. I bet it looked something like it did at graduation when you told him you would not be going to work at Nelson Records."

Wait a minute, how did he know that? He was dead when I graduated college.

"How..."

"I was there. I couldn't miss your graduation. I was also at your wedding. Lucas was a cocksucker. It was hard not to strangle him after you told me what he was doing, all that cheating. He is not a man by the way. Men do not cheat on their wives."

He was there.

For some reason that made me feel good, knowing that he cared enough to not miss important days in my life.

I was quickly running through my options. I

knew Shane. He was going to try and railroad me any minute. I had to have a plan before he did. What did I have in my life I couldn't live without? My centers were the only thing I would miss. The only thing I truly loved in this world, next to Shane. What was important was the work that the centers did, not me running them. Rebecca was ready, she had helped me manage them the last two years. There was absolutely nothing here for me except loneliness and regret. My biggest regret, of course, was not telling Shane I loved him before he left on deployment, that I didn't fight for him because I was a chicken shit.

I had nothing left to lose. I had lived twelve years without him. Oh shit, what if in the last twelve years he had found someone? Someone he loved. I didn't think he was married or had kids due to his speech about protecting me.

"Is there someone...a woman...I mean, do you love someone?" I hid my face in my hands. How embarrassing, I was a grown woman for Christ sakes, and I couldn't ask a simple question. I was behaving like I was sixteen again. "God, I'm an idiot."

"Yes, I am in love with someone," he answered.

Damn, that hurt. Like, really hurt. A thousand sharp knives pierced my heart. I couldn't even look at him. I kept my face in my hands and tried my hardest not to cry. Of course he was. How stupid could I be? I was just his childhood friend he was trying to keep safe. There was never anything more between us. He kissed me one time. Probably just nervous about going on his first deployment. It certainly didn't mean to him what it meant to me.

New plan.

"Who was shooting at us?" I asked, needing to change the subject.

"I don't know. I called it in, but I haven't heard back with an ID yet," he responded.

"Okay. So *why* were they shooting at us? And was it you or me they were shooting at?"

"I won't have a definitive answer on that until I hear back from Command. Best guess, they were going to take you to get to me. If they were smart, they would've kept you alive long enough to bring me in. Killing you before they had me would've resulted in the opposite reaction they wanted."

"What does that mean? Opposite reaction."

"It means I would hunt down every person that had to do with your death and slit their throats."

I swallowed the lump in my throat. I don't know if that was the most disturbing thing I'd ever heard or the most romantic.

"What does this mean for me now that they know I exist? Do I have to die too and go somewhere new?" I continued to question him.

I didn't want to leave my centers if I didn't have to. Shane belonged to someone else, and I would need the distraction. This was going to be like going back to square one. The mourning and pain would start all over again. Only this time it was with the knowledge he was somewhere out there and he was choosing not to have anything to do with me. At least before I believed he was dead. There would be no more visiting the cemetery talking to him. He would truly be gone.

"Lily? Aren't you gonna ask me who I am in love with? Who this woman is?" he asked.

Hell to the no. I didn't want to know anything about her. I couldn't even muster up a fake smile and a polite congratulations. I was trying not to choke as I held back my tears. There was only so much I could take.

Vibration under my ass made me jump, and I banged my elbow on the steering wheel.

"Ouch." I rubbed my elbow and moved over so he could get his phone out of his pocket.

"Go for Lenox," he answered and paused before

continuing. "Copy that. We'll be in. ETA is four hours," Shane said.

"What's Lenox?" I asked.

"Not a what, a who. I'm Lenox. Carter Lenox," Shane explained.

Holy shit, he used my middle name as his alias. Why would he do that?

"It's too much. I can't..." my body shook uncontrollably, and the tears poured down my cheeks. "I can't lose you again. I don't think I'll make it a second time."

8

She was trembling in my arms. I had only ever seen Lily this upset at my funeral. And even then, she hid it well. I did this to her. All of it. Twelve years' worth of pain and heartache. And now I was doing it some more. What a bastard I was. I should never have told her I was in love with someone. It was only going to make leaving her again harder. And as much as I would rather die a thousand painful deaths than cause her any more grief, it had to be done.

The fact still remained I lived a dangerous life. She was my only weakness. If something happened to her, it would be my downfall. I didn't know what the right answer was. My brain was telling me I had to take her back to the compound and quickly get her a new identity and have her set up in a new location, one I knew nothing about.

But my heart was telling me to keep her close and protect her myself. But what would happen the next time I went on a mission? She'd be a sitting duck. This was fucked. These were the unknown effects of my decision to join the 707.

"I'm so sorry. I know that my decisions have hurt you. I wish there was some way to take that all away. But I can't. I am a selfish prick, I chose my job and still couldn't give you up. Not completely."

"How could you do that to me? You left me," she yelled.

I stopped and stared into her glistening eyes, wet with tears. My hands moved on their own accord going to her neck and feeling the soft skin there. *Feeling.* For the first time in years, I actually felt a woman's skin. My hands continued their ascent, cupping her face in my palms. So smooth and warm. Her eyes closed and her head tilted to the side, rubbing her cheek against my work rough hand.

She looked so damn beautiful even in her anger. I brought my lips to hers. What was supposed to be a soft touching of the lips, an apology of sorts, quickly became something more. Her tongue came out and licked the seam of my lips, and she moaned against my mouth.

I pulled away startled. The electricity snapping between us was unbelievable. A simple lick of my lips had my body standing at attention ready to take her.

"Did you feel that?" she asked. Her eyes dancing with heat.

"I did," I confirmed.

We met somewhere in the middle as we both leaned in for more. Our lips collided and our tongues tangled together. Nothing had ever felt so good. Even the kiss in the hotel room in Georgia wasn't this. That first kiss was full of regret and sorrow. I knew what I had done. I knew I was leaving her. This kiss was full of heat and passion. Love and lust that knew no bounds.

Her hands went under my shirt, and her nails scored my skin as she dragged them up my stomach.

"Holy shit," she murmured with her lips still on mine. "I need this off," she demanded, tugging at my shirt.

I pulled my shirt over my head and tossed it on the passenger seat. Her eyes widened in appreciation as she took in my bare chest. A heartbeat later her shirt joined mine, and her full tits bounced, still partially covered by the pink lacy bra she wore. Even with the obstructed view, I could see her nipples were hard and straining against the fabric.

"This too. Take this off." She fumbled with the zipper of my jeans.

Abandoning her attempt to undress me, she went for the button of her own shorts. She rolled to the side, sitting on the center console, and in one smooth motion she pulled off her shorts and panties. My jeans were barely open when she straddled my lap and her slick pussy nestled against my dick.

I ran my hands up her thighs - so damn soft. "I missed you, Lily."

"Don't say that. Just fuck me, Shane. No more talking." She took my mouth, silencing me.

The passion and lust were still present, but there was an underlying presence of urgency. She said fuck her - not make love to her, not have sex. If I was a better man, I would've put a stop to this. But I wasn't, and the need to finally have her was overwhelming. I knew what this was; she was using me to work off some of the fear, shock, and anger still pulsing through her. I understood that all too well. How many times had I used meaningless women to do the same? I only wished I wasn't that to her, that this could've meant something more, and I could've been the man she deserved.

But I wasn't, and she viewed this as a quick fuck to make her feel alive.

I positioned my dick at her entrance, and she slid down taking me inside of her. The lace of her bra chafed my chest as she glided herself up and down my dick. That had to go; I needed to watch her tits bounce in my face. I unclipped the back and yanked it free. Goddamn her tits were amazing. I licked and sucked and touched everywhere. Every place I had dreamt about. My hands found her tight ass, and I squeezed and massaged, helping her ride me faster. She was grinding herself against me on every down stroke sending bolts of pleasure through my body. Her snug pussy was so fucking wet, her excitement was coating my balls - this was going to be a lot faster than I wanted.

"I need you to get there, Lily," I demanded.

"Almost," she panted. Her lips went back to my neck, her teeth digging into my skin.

She slammed down on my dick and rocked herself back and forth, grinding herself so hard she had me seeing stars.

"Now, baby. You have to come now." I pushed deeper and rocked her faster.

It was a goddamn miracle when her pussy convulsed and tightened around my dick. There was nothing I could do to stop myself from coming. My body tensed and I let go, enjoying the rush of pleasure.

Lily stilled, her lips still at my neck, kissing the sting of her bite. The girl was a vampire - she had to have left marks. Not that I gave two shits. I would enjoy looking at them. They would be a beautiful reminder of what I lost once she was gone.

I was enjoying the feel of her back as I traced the bumps of her spine when she spoke, "What now?"

I didn't want to talk about what now. I wanted to enjoy her relaxed against me, my stiff dick still inside of her.

"Lily."

"I know you want to get rid of me," she whispered.

"No, I don't want to get rid of you. I want you safe," I corrected.

"Why can't you keep me safe? Maybe this is our second chance. I have loved you since I was sixteen. I'm not ready to lose you again."

Lily's admission gutted me. Her tears on my chest rolled over my heart. Like an indelible mark, I would forever feel them on my skin. I would wear her tears for the rest of my life.

"I can't protect you if you're with me. A good operator and a good husband cannot be saddled in the same man. I have to be one or the other. The only way for me to keep you safe is if you are far away from me."

I cannot believe that fucked-up garbage just came out of my mouth. I was lying to us both. I knew plenty of men who worked with me that were married. Maybe I am still the weak coward I was at twenty. I had a choice, I could've brought her with me.

But I didn't. And now I was about to pay the ultimate price.

9

He was as much fool as he was stubborn if he thought I wasn't going to fight for us. I refused to live with any more regrets. It had taken me years and a whole lot of soul searching to change my life from a rich spoiled twit to someone I could be proud of.

There was nothing harder than taking a look in the mirror with an honest eye and admitting your shortcomings. Picking yourself apart and having the audacity to make a change. I did that. I did the hard work. And I'll be damned if I lived out the rest of my life lonely because I gave up.

Unfortunately, I couldn't convince him here in the car. I was in no position to argue while I was still naked on his lap. I was so bloody mad at him. All that anger bubbled up, and it had nowhere to go. So

I used him to fuck it out of me. Not that he seemed to mind. If nothing more, I would have the memory of us being together one time. I wasn't naïve - I didn't have my head in the clouds with unicorns dancing around me. I knew I had a fight on my hands and it was a long shot I could convince him not to leave me again. But the operative word was *fight*, and I was going to fight until there was nothing left.

"Where are you supposed to be taking me?" I asked.

"Shit. We have to go. If we don't check in within the next four hours, Command will send out a rescue team. Come on, we have to hurry."

I pushed off his chest, and my eyes slowly ate up the view. I had never seen muscles like his in real life. His chest and abs were cut, every muscle fully defined. I glanced farther down at where our bodies were still connected, and my pussy tightened.

His dick twitched in response, and he let out a low growl.

"We don't have time for round two, and my cock is still throbbing hard inside of you." He pulled me by the hair and pressed his firm lips against mine in a soft peck before he gently kissed my forehead. "Hop up, we have to go."

I opened my eyes from the kiss, and the charm around his neck caught my attention.

"Is this mine?" I asked.

"Yeah, I took it while you were in Georgia," he admitted.

"I thought I lost it. I went crazy looking for it and was heartbroken when it never turned up."

Shane had bought me a beautiful silver tree of life necklace one day when we were walking along the Venice boardwalk. I loved that necklace and wore it every day until it went missing.

"I needed to take a piece of you with me. I haven't taken it off since the day I took it," he explained.

I gently fingered the charm, happy he had something of mine with him all these years. It meant he thought of me.

Reality came crashing down on me when I remembered he said he was in love with someone. I couldn't believe how irrationally jealous I was at the thought of him wearing my necklace while loving someone else.

Oh God, we had sex.

My stomach rolled, and I felt sick. How could I've been so stupid and get caught up in the moment? We were no better than our cheating parents.

I scrambled off his lap, disgusted with myself when I pulled off his dick and all but jumped into the passenger seat. I found my shorts and quickly pulled them up my legs sans panties and did the same with my shirt. Wordlessly, I threw his shirt in his lap trying to cover the evidence of our indiscretion.

"What's wrong? I'm sorry about the necklace," he started.

"Fuck the necklace. I thought we were in a hurry." I angrily adjusted my shirt trying to regain some sort of modesty, which was hard with large boobs and no bra.

"We're not going anywhere until you tell me what's wrong. Shit girl, you just went from riding my dick to prickly in one point two seconds." He reached across and stilled my hands as they needlessly pulled at the hem of my shirt.

"Nice, Shane. You wanna know what's wrong? You're in love with another woman and fucked me without giving her another thought. That's what's fucking wrong," I yelled.

"Oh that. Believe me, I was thinking about her the whole time I was fucking you," he told me with a cockiness I had never seen in him before.

Bile rushed up, and I thought I was going to throw up.

"You're a disgusting pig. How dare you say that to me?"

"There isn't a single moment of the day I don't think about her. And when you were riding my cock and your tits bouncing in my face, the only thing I could think of was her. And how long I had waited to feel her, and taste her, and how my fucking soul was finally home."

"Feel her? What the hell, Shane." I wanted to be angry but I couldn't - I was too devastated.

"It's you, Lily. I have loved you for what feels like my whole life. I have never loved another woman, and I never will. Remember when we were at the Observatory looking at the stars and I told you that I knew there was only one person out there I was meant to love? And when I gave my love to her it would be hers forever? I knew then, that person was you."

"Then you left me. Alone. To mourn your death. You left, and I became everything we hated because I was weak. You left, and I was forced to marry a man who lied and cheated on me. I hated myself for disappointing you."

"You're right, I did do that." He stopped to pull

his shirt over his head and started to fix his pants. I won't lie, I watched as he tucked his dick back in his pants and wished I had savored those last moments with him a little more.

"But I did it for your safety. Don't you understand that you could've been taken today or killed? What if I wasn't there? What if those men had come to the center and took you? That is why I faked my death. My father was too high profile - I would've been easy to track, it would've been a cakewalk for these douche bags to find you."

Suddenly I was bone tired and didn't feel like hashing this out. As much as I hated to admit it, he was right. If he hadn't been there today, I could've been hurt or killed. Was I willing to live in constant fear that something could happen to me or to him? That was a question I wasn't ready to think about at the moment.

"We should go. And thank you, by the way, for saving me from those men." I looked out the passenger window as Shane started the car and slowly started to drive down the dirt access road.

It had been a long time since I was up here at the reservoir. We used to come here a lot with our friends when we were in high school. It was much different then. There weren't houses or boat docks. It was basically abandoned back in the day.

I closed my eyes and welcomed the silence. I just wanted a few minutes to rest my racing thoughts.

It's not every day your best friend comes back from the dead.

10

Over the course of the three-and-a-half-hour drive, I stole sideways glances at Lily while she slept. She looked so beautiful. It was surreal having her sit next to me. Doing something as mundane as driving in a car together, I never thought we'd do that again. Never thought we would have another conversation.

I missed her so much over the last twelve years. There were so many times I wanted to pick up the phone and call her. There were some dark and lonely times where I needed to hear her voice but forced myself to wait. Knowing that I would see her on the anniversary of my death and hear her voice was what got me through. Each year that passed, I became more and more worried she wouldn't show up. I was deathly afraid she would move on and not come to see me anymore. Some years she came later in the day than others. My gut would be in knots as I sat there waiting. Then I'd see her, and my whole body would relax.

She was my church; her sweet words washed the past years' sins clean. I could leave the cemetery and go back to work with a clean slate. If God allowed me another year on earth to see her again, then I knew I must've been forgiven.

All too soon we turned down a long dirt road that ran parallel to the Twenty-Nine Palms runway, and the rundown hangar came into view. This area was almost deserted; it was the perfect place for a low-key hideaway.

I didn't want to bring her here. I wanted to run away with her to that little island off Croatia and pretend I hadn't left her all those years ago. I wanted her all to myself.

"Lily. We're here." I tried to wake her.

She shifted in her sleep, turning her face toward me but kept her eyes closed. I put the car in park and took one last look at her before I had to take her into the lion's den. Her eyelashes gently fanned across her skin, her brow completely relaxed in slumber. She looked so at peace.

As much as I didn't want to, I had to rip the

band-aid off and get this over with. The longer she was with me, the more I started to believe I could keep her.

"Time to wake up," I called out and gently shook her.

She awoke with a start, but her face quickly gentled, her eyes coming to mine.

"I thought it was a dream. A really, really great dream," she whispered. "What's gonna happen to me now?"

"I won't know until after I've been briefed," I answered.

"I'm scared. Are they gonna take me away from you?"

There was no telling what was going to happen once we went into the hangar. I didn't want to scare her even more than she already was, but depending on who those men were, there was a possibility she would be taken underground immediately.

"There's nothing to be afraid of," I lied.

She was smart to be scared. This right here was why I faked my death - to free her from the burden of fear.

"I trust you."

Fuck. I didn't deserve those words.

"Let's get you inside."

I hurried her into the hangar anxious to see what my team had found. When we entered, all eyes came to us. Clark and Jasper looked up from the pictures they had spread out over a large wood table. Levi glanced up over the five-computer screens in front of him, but continued to type furiously on the keyboard.

"'Bout time you made it in," Clark greeted. "Took your sweet ass time."

"What can I say? Traffic was a bitch," I answered.

Levi stopped typing and walked over to us. "You must be Lillian. I'm Levi, nice to meet you."

Levi extended his hand. Before Lily reached for it, she looked up at me, and I nodded my head in encouragement.

"Lily, please. Nice to meet you, Levi," Lily said shaking his hand.

"That's Clark and Jasper." I made the introductions.

Jasper looked her over, a sly appreciative smile started to form. "So, this is Lily, huh?" Jasper said as he continued to eye her.

"Jasper..." I said in warning. I didn't like the way he was staring at her; like she was some barfly he was getting ready to score with.

"Shane, it's okay." Her hand came to mine and gave it a squeeze before she let go and walked to Jasper.

"It's nice to meet you, Jasper. I'd like to say I've heard great things about you, but the truth is he's zipped up tighter than a nun and never mentioned you." With a wink, she extended her hand.

Jasper stared at her before he looked down at her extended hand. He threw his head back and busted out laughing. It had taken several seconds before he regained his composure. Without warning, he pushed her hand away and pulled her into a hug.

This was not going to go well for my friend if he continued to touch my girl. Wait! What the fuck, Lily was not my girl. That was the kind of thinking that was going to get me in trouble.

"Jesus, that was fuckin' funny. Welcome to the hangar. The accommodations suck ass, but we do have good whiskey and coffee. Would you like either?" Jasper continued to chuckle.

"I'll have a bottle of water if you have any. And I'll take you up on that whiskey as soon as I find out if I'm dead or not," Lily teased.

"Yeah, I like you. We'll get along just fine. I can set you up with a laptop, and you can pick out your coffin just in case the need arises."

I didn't like Jasper getting so friendly with Lily. I should've been happy she was being so easygoing and agreeable. Most women would've been throwing a temper tantrum by now. But not Lily. Here she was smiling and trying to put on a brave face. I still didn't like the flirtation in her tone, but it was better than the alternative.

Clark was standing back watching and had yet to engage. That was him - ever watchful. Clark never rushed into any situation, he always hung back and observed before he made any judgments.

All joking subsided when she turned to Clark and squared her shoulders. "You must be Clark. I'm sorry for all the trouble I caused."

"No trouble, ma'am. If you'd like, Lenox can show you to one of the bunk rooms, and you can rest." I noticed he didn't extend his hand to shake hers. He was also formal with her. What the hell was that about?

"If it's all the same to you, sir, I'd prefer to stay where Sha...Lenox can keep watch over me. I mean no disrespect, but I do not know any of you. I'm sure you understand. I can sit in the corner, I promise not to be in the way."

Clark eyed her carefully and nodded his head,

"Understandable. And smart. Lenox, get your girl comfortable. We'll brief in five."

"Is that Mr. Kincaid?" Lily asked, pointing to one of the photographs on the table.

"This?" Clark picked up the picture and held it out for Lily to inspect.

"Yes. That's Calvin Kincaid. Why do you have all these pictures of him?"

"You're positive this is Calvin Kincaid?" Clark asked.

"Yes, he is one of my donors." She looked at Clark confused.

"Levi, pull up Calvin Kincaid, full work-up. Jasper, please get Mrs. Nordoff a bottle of water. Lenox, pull all of the McGrath Carter financials. I want everything dating back from when the doors opened."

I didn't miss Lily's flinch when Clark called her by her married name. He knew that wasn't her name. He also knew that would upset her. She had changed her name back to Nelson as soon as she divorced that scumbag.

What did he find while we were driving in? I hated not having all the information, and I really didn't appreciate Clark blindsiding me.

"If you don't mind, my name is Lily. But if you

insist on being formal, Ms. Nelson will do. Surely a man with your intelligence and access to information would've known that. So, if that was your attempt to unnerve me, you'll need to try harder.

"I am happy to tell you anything you'd like to know about Calvin Kincaid, as he seems to be of importance to you." Lily stopped and turned to me. "If you'd like my financials for the centers, I can give you my banking login and the codes to dial into the hard drive. Or I suppose you could hack in yourself, whatever way is faster for you."

I didn't appreciate Clark treating her like a target, and I really didn't like that he was trying to put her on edge.

"I'll take your login codes. Has Kincaid made any sizeable donations?" I asked.

"Sizable? No. He makes monthly donations, a wire of five thousand dollars. He has given larger sums when I've solicited money for a fundraiser," Lily explained.

"Sixty grand a year sounds pretty sizable," Clark whistled.

"I assume you know my upbringing. I would further assume you know my personal financial status. Sixty thousand dollars a year to a charity is a drop in the bucket. So, no, sixty grand is not sizeable," Lily snarled.

"And why would you assume that?"

Christ, I had to put an end to this pissing match.

"Back off, Clark."

"I'm fine, Lenox. Those assumptions are based on the fact you strike me as a man who does his homework. The same way I wouldn't walk into a room full of investors without knowing all there was to know about them. You've had four hours to dig through my life. I'm sure you did it well. I am an open book, Clark. All you have to do is ask."

"I have done my homework. And some things are not adding up," Clark shot back.

"What the fuck are you talking about, Clark?" I asked.

"Why don't you tell me about Kincaid." Clark ignored me and continue to address Lily.

"Do you mind if I sit?" She waited for Clark to motion to the chair. "Let's see, I met him at a movie premiere in New York about eighteen-ish months ago. He asked me out to dinner."

The growl that was bubbling up must've escaped because Lily looked at me and Jasper chuckled. Asshole.

"Sorry, continue," I urged.

"I declined his offer. Over the course of the evening, a producer friend mentioned to Calvin that I ran a charity in Los Angeles. Calvin asked for my card and said he'd like to make a donation. I gave him my card, and that was the last I saw of him that evening. About a week later he showed up at my Northridge center and asked for a tour. I gave him one, and he asked me out again for dinner and drinks. Again, I declined. He seemed to take it well. He then said he would like to set up monthly deposits. We went to my office so I could give him the banking information for his financial advisor, and that was it. He thanked me for my time and left."

"Who was the producer?" I asked.

"Clyde Davison. I'm sure you remember him. Your father worked on one of his movies."

I turned the name over in my mind and recognition dawned. "Yes, I remember him. He was with Sommers Studio, he arranged financing. Slimy bastard was always trying to find creative ways to fund the studio's films, like scamming people."

"And since then? Have you seen Kincaid again?" Clark questioned.

"Yes, I have seen him at various functions in Los Angeles. I think at a breast cancer event, and maybe an awards show. Neither time did he speak to me, he simply acknowledged me with a wave. And he also sent in a fifty-thousand-dollar donation in lieu of attending a fundraiser for a new gymnasium in our Oxnard center."

"You never went to dinner or drinks with Kincaid? No personal involvement at all?" he continued.

"I said I didn't. Are you questioning my veracity?"

Clark studied Lily for a moment. I wasn't sure where he was going with this, but I really didn't fucking like how he was badgering her.

"Not at all, I am simply trying to make sure you've remembered every interaction you've had with him."

"I'll be honest. I didn't realize I needed to be paying attention and taking notes at every event I attended over the last eighteen months." Lily stopped and blew out a breath. Her shoulders sagged forward, and she suddenly looked worn out. "You have to understand something, Clark, I hate going to these events. I despise pretentious assholes who think because they are the Hollywood elite they get to behave however they please. I am nervous when I go because I have to turn into one of them. I have to be Lillian Nelson, and I do it because I want money to keep my centers up and running. I deeply struggle with that, then I remember my centers help people. People who need it. So when I attend these events, I am nervous and annoyed the whole time I am there." Lily stopped again and took a deep breath. "I am a fake, a complete fraud. I go, I pretend I am one of them to fit in, then I leave. But, I can assure you, I have never gone on a date or had any personal interaction with Calvin Kincaid."

"Have you ever seen him on the street or the grocery store. Anywhere like that?"

"Enough Clark. She answered your goddamn questions," I exploded. "She's not a fucking target."

"She is, Lenox. Just not ours," Clark shot back and handed me a stack of pictures of Lily.

"What the fuck are these?" I asked, spreading them across the table.

Lily. At least twenty different pictures of her coming out of a variety of places: the supermarket, a clothing boutique, inside one of her centers. She was never looking at the camera. Someone was tailing her.

"Oh my God," she whispered.

"Where in the hell did you get these?"

"Those were on a compact flash card in a camera that was found in the car of one of the suits today,"

Clark answered, keeping his eyes diverted. That was his tell, he would never look at you when he was hiding something. The irony wasn't lost on me. He was the best operator I knew. When we were in the field, he was ice, but with the team he couldn't hide shit.

"What else?" I asked.

Clark remained silent looking at the pictures.

"Tell him. He needs to know," Jasper said from behind me.

"We sent Hesh to Lily's place. We wanted her house scrubbed as quickly as possible. There were cameras."

Tears fell from her eyes, and she lost the battle, breaking down and crying into her hands.

I tried to hold on to my temper. The last thing I wanted was Lily seeing this side of me. The cold, detached Carter Lenox. I'd hoped she would never meet him. But in the end, I couldn't contain my rage.

"I am going to find him and slit his goddamn throat." I exploded.

11

Shane detonated and slammed both fists on the tables, shocking me into silence. I had never, not once, seen him lose his temper like this. This man before me was not my Shane, he was someone else entirely. This man, Lenox, scared me.

"Why are there cameras in my house?" I asked.

I was a nobody. No one cared enough about me to watch me, not even my father cared that much.

"It means someone has been watching you. Twelve fucking years for nothing. Goddamn it," Shane shouted.

"Lenox, calm the fuck down. You're scaring Lily," Clark chastised.

"I'm scaring Lily? She should be fucking scared; an arms dealer has had her under surveillance."

Shane's face contorted before he continued, "Did Hesh find out where the network feeds were stored?"

"Arms dealer? Who is an arms dealer?" I asked.

"He did. They went directly to an office space in La Brea leased under the name Calvin Kincaid. I'll tell you what, that asshole Roman has balls," Clark answered, ignoring me.

"Who is Roman?" I tried interrupting Clark and Shane.

"That's too easy. The fucker wanted us to make the connection. He is taunting me, sending a message that he knows about Lily. What else did he find?" Shane asked Clark, shifting the photographs around on the table.

"Agreed, he could've had that routed..."

"I asked a damn question," I yelled.

"What?" Shane snapped, looking at me as if he had forgotten I was even in the room.

"Who is an arms dealer? And who is Roman? I thought you said Calvin Kincaid leased the office," I repeated my earlier questions.

A chill ran through my body just thinking about someone watching me. I was trying to put on a brave face in front of Shane, but inside I was freaking out. Some stranger had been watching me. Taking pictures of me. I didn't even want to ask if there were cameras in my bedroom. The thought of that made me want to pass out.

As hard as I tried, I couldn't keep up with what they were talking about. Roman, Calvin Kincaid, routing camera feeds. Jeez. They needed to slow down and start explaining what was going on.

"Everything will be fine, Lily. Why don't you get that bottle of water and go relax," Shane suggested.

"You're kidding, right? Please tell me you are joking. Someone has been following me and taking pictures of me, and you tell me to go get a bottle of water? Don't do that to me, don't dismiss me like everyone else in my life."

I hated that shit. My father had done that to me for as long as I could remember. He blew me off every chance he could. Unless he needed to parade me around some stupid function, he couldn't be bothered to answer even the simplest questions or spare me a second of his precious time.

"I am not dismissing you. But this is not some silly charity benefit or fundraiser. We are talking national security and criminal cartels, Lily. I don't have time to fuck around and explain things to you. Besides, you can't even know the details without a security clearance."

Ouch. His words hurt worse than all the times

my father had dismissed me combined. I fought to hold back the tears.

"I'm not asking you to divulge state secrets, asshole. But I do have the right to know who has been following me and why. I have a right to know if the bastard videotaped me naked in my bedroom," I squared my shoulders and prayed my voice sounded braver than I felt.

Shane growled and punched the table again. "That's where you are wrong..."

"Easy, Lenox. Jesus. She is right, you know. She needs to know who she has been doing business with and who has been following her. You need to get your shit straight. You're too emotionally involved," Jasper weighed in, cutting Shane off from further insulting me.

"Roman and Calvin Kincaid are the same person. He is a munitions dealer. I don't know if meeting you at the premiere was by chance or it was a setup. We are still digging into the Calvin Kincaid alias and associates." Clark started to explain, showing me side-by-side pictures of Calvin Kincaid in a tux and Roman in what looks like army fatigues. "Which leaves the question of how long and why he has had you under surveillance," he continued. "Maybe he thought Lenox still visited you and he could easily take him out. Or maybe he wanted intel before he decided what to do with you. Hell, if the man was smart, just sending Lenox a single picture of you would've sent him spiraling out of control. As he is currently demonstrating." Clark cut his eyes to Shane. "Imagine if you weren't standing here now. If he didn't know if you were okay or not, he would've lost his mind and abandoned a mission to go find you."

Sweet Jesus, that was a lot of information to process, but my mind was stuck on the part about taking Shane out. He had told me his job was dangerous. I wasn't completely naïve, I had seen all the Navy SEAL action movies. I had a good idea what he did, but stupidly I was hoping he had been exaggerating.

I should've been more worried knowing a criminal was following me and taking pictures, but I couldn't begin to process that part. I needed to be alone where I could break down without anyone seeing me. I couldn't show any weakness in front of these men. They had to think I was just as mentally resilient as them, that someone stalking me and invading my privacy didn't bother me. I had spent my whole life putting on a front. I was a master at concealing my emotions.

"Let me see all the pictures, and I'll try and tell you when some of them were taken. Would that help?" I asked Clark. Shoring up my defenses, I chanced a look at Shane.

He did indeed look like he'd lost his mind. I was pissed and wanted to tell him to screw off, but this man in front of me did not look like a man you fucked with.

"It would." Clark started to spread the photographs out over the table. "Can you tell me more about when Kincaid came to the center?"

Shane stomped away like a petulant child not getting his way. Inside I was secretly happy he was pissed too. My feelings were hurt, and I wanted him to feel just as annoyed as I was. Stupid bastard. He knew how badly it hurt me when I was treated like I was useless. His snide comment about the situation not being a silly charity event didn't go unnoticed. That's what he thought of me, that I was another spoiled Hollywood brat who had a cause to fill her pointless days.

"Sure." I thought back to the day Calvin showed up. "You know, I was surprised to see him because he said he lived in the Bahamas. He bragged about his private island in the Exumas. He went on and on to the point of ad nauseam about the house and staff he kept. As if he was impressing me with his money. Sorry, back to the center. Nothing out of the ordinary. He asked me for a tour but didn't seem all that interested, it was very obvious he had ulterior motives."

"And what do you think his motives were?" Clark inquired.

"Well, he walked very close to me and flirted when he could. He was over-the-top charming to the point of being transparent about his reasons for visiting me. He didn't seem to care about my center; he was sucking up. When he asked me out again, it confirmed my suspicions. I assume the only reason he even wanted to donate any money was to save face after I rebuffed his advances again. Then I took him to my office...oh my God."

"What?" Clark stood up looking at the picture I had in my hand.

"My office. I have pictures of Shane and me from high school, his basic training graduation, and the trip from before his deployment. Calvin asked me about them."

"Fuck," Shane roared. "What did you say?"

"Swear to God, Lenox I am gonna lock your ass down if you don't calm the fuck down," Clark shouted back.

"Twelve goddamn years for nothing," Shane mumbled under his breath.

"I am so sorry. I didn't know. I would never have kept those pictures if I had known you were really alive galivanting around the world playing Captain America. How was I supposed to know you weren't really dead?"

"Lily, you didn't do anything wrong. When Shane went underground, the military scrubbed everything they could. But it doesn't matter how good of a job they do, it is always the innocent slip that breaks the cover. Does that make sense?" Clark's demeanor had changed toward me. His body language was no longer hostile, and his tone had softened.

"No, I don't really understand any of this," I answered honestly. "I think I need that whiskey now. I'm so freaking confused."

"Okay. The military can't control the human factor. Shane Owings is dead. But there are still photographs of him out there; the military can't take all those back. You did nothing wrong. This is just one of those times we all hope never happens - when our past catches up with us."

"I told Calvin about Shane. That he was my best friend," I whispered.

"Did he ask any other questions?" Clark questioned.

"Yes, he asked what he did in the Army, and how he died. I told him that too."

"Again, you did nothing wrong. Someone asked you about a friend that died, you answered. The good news is that your answers would've been natural, and your pain real. You didn't have to put on an act or give a practiced response. Someone like Roman would've picked up on that in two point five seconds."

"What now?"

"Now I hunt and kill the bastard," Shane declared.

12

My mind was reeling. How the hell had Roman found Lily? I very rarely believed in dumb luck or coincidences, but this seemed to be one of those one in a million instances. The stars aligned and he got lucky.

Son of a bitch, all those years flushed down the toilet. The pain I have caused her was all for naught.

I was pacing, and my hands were itching to kill. This was not going to be a nice clean death, I was going to strangle him with my bare hands and watch the life fade from his eyes. We had been chasing Roman for the last seven years. He was always one step ahead of us. His ammunition and guns have killed countless innocent people and an untold number of service men and women. He deserved it – a slow painful death.

"The Bahama line is gonna take a while. The Bahamian government is shit at keeping records if you have money. And there are too many ways in and out of the islands. The government gives zero fucks about seaplanes and yachts, it is a runners' paradise down there," Levi informed the room. He looked up from his monitors and addressed Lily, "Did Kincaid happen to tell you the name of his island? Any landmarks, location in the Exumas, anything? There are over three hundred cays that make up the game preserve."

My gut was still turning, all the ways I tried to keep her safe was for nothing. Everything I tried to prevent from happening was unfolding. Not only was she in danger, we now needed information from her, further involving her in an investigation I wanted her nowhere near.

Roman was ruthless. He had nothing to lose, he cared about nothing. He wouldn't think twice about disposing of Lily in the most horrific way possible now that he knew she meant something to me. Lily was the chink in my armor he was looking for. Now he would exploit it.

"Nothing I can think of. He did prattle on about

his environmental concern and how he was trying to go green on his cay. I believe he said he has windmills. But, honestly, it sounded like he was trying to impress me, so I wasn't paying attention. He never mentioned a name."

"That's a start. Any small detail will help," Levi told her.

Clark kept cutting sideways glances at me. He looked like he had something to say, but he kept his lips pinched tight and eyes thoughtful. He was really starting to piss me off; one minute he was grilling Lily giving her the third degree, and now he was treating her like an honorary member of the team, telling her information she had no business knowing.

Lily and Clark continued to look over the pictures, and Levi was digging up everything he could on Kincaid. That left me to shift through Lily's personal financial records and McGrath Carter bank accounts.

The day Lily sat at my grave and told me about the center she had opened, my heart swelled with pride. She was giving and thoughtful; she always had been, but this went beyond that to complete selflessness. She had used her own personal trust to fund the centers until she could get a steady stream of donor money. And when she divorced that bastard

Lucas, she sunk every penny of the settlement into opening more centers or improving the ones already opened.

More than that, she gave the people who needed the services of the centers her time. And not just the back-end fundraising - she tutored, delivered food, and drove the van to take the kids on excursions. The girl was something else.

I needed to push thoughts of Lily aside and concentrate on how Roman became Calvin Kincaid and why. I looked at Levi who had maps of the Exumas pulled up on his monitors.

"Hey, you gotta minute to talk this through?" I asked. Too much wasn't adding up.

"Yep." He turned his chair giving me his attention.

"Why would Roman donate money to McGrath Carter?" I started.

"To get close to Lily," he answered.

"She had already turned down his advances, yet he continued to give money. We both know that asshole doesn't have an altruistic bone in his body."

"Maybe he meant to only give money once, to save face after Lily turned him down. Once he saw your picture in her office, he continued to give money monthly to fuck with us. Show us that he has had long term contact with her and he could've taken her out at any point. Get in our heads," Levi theorized.

"Okay, that makes sense. Now, what about the initial meeting? The introduction from Clyde Davidson. How and why did Roman get involved in the movie industry?" I asked.

"Launder money? You said that Davidson secured financing for studios. If Roman gave his ill-begotten gains to the studio and the production made money, it would come out clean on the other side." Levi leaned back in his chair and stretched his long legs out in front of him.

"That could work. But the movie industry is risky. You can lose your ass if a film doesn't make money at the box office," I explained.

"Let's look at this another way. Roman went rogue and left Command after his wife died. Why did he leave?" Levi asked.

"Man, we have gone over his motives a hundred times in the last seven years. He lost his shit when his wife killed herself. He blamed Command for not cutting loose and prosecuting the Sergeant Major who was having an affair with Melanie," I answered.

"Who knew about the affair?"

"We all did. Hell, the entire unit knew that Melanie was fucking that prick."

It was the worst kept secret around the 707. Melanie was not stealthy in her goings and comings. She didn't give a shit if everyone knew, and she borderline shoved Roman's face in it.

"Right, so he was pissed at all of us when he left. We have pinpointed that was his motivation for selling secrets and weapons that would be used to kill American troops. But what if it is us specifically he wants revenge on? Did he know about your life before the 707?"

"Fuck." I shot up from my seat and started pacing again. "There was one time a few years after my death I was so goddamn screwed in the head after I saw Lily at the cemetery. I was drunk and flapping at the gums, questioning everything I had done. I mean, I had given up the one thing I loved. Roman asked why I chose to get a new identity, he hadn't and he was part of the 707. I told him that it was because my father was high profile and easily found. I was drunk, I don't remember if I told a trusted member of my team if he was in the film industry. But I know for a fact that I never mentioned Lily's name. After my funeral, I never said her name out loud again - it hurt too fucking bad."

I heard a sob from across the room, and I closed my eyes. I couldn't look at her, I didn't want to see the pain that I knew was there. I'd screwed up again and got carried away saying shit she never needed to hear.

"Lily," I started. I needed to fix this somehow.

"Don't. Don't say a word to me. You led me to believe that all of you had changed your identities," she hissed.

"No, I didn't. I never told you that. I told you I faked my death to protect you, and I did. You think I gave a rat's ass if something would've happened to that bastard father of mine or the cheating bitch of a mother? As cold as you may think this makes me, I would've looked the other way. You are the only thing I cared about. Do you know how easy it would've been for any of the scumbags we chase to find Shane Owings, the son of an Academy Award winning actor, and think they had found the holy grail of operators to capture? When the 707 suggested that Shane Owings should die and Carter Lenox would be born in his place, I jumped at the chance."

"You didn't ask me if I wanted to be protected," she fired back.

"Fuck no, I didn't. I knew you'd follow me. And every time I would have left for a mission, you'd sit at home and worry if I was coming back. I wanted better for you. I wanted you to be happy and at peace. Somewhere safe, where my choices didn't bleed into your life."

"I would've followed you. I would've supported your choices, and I would've given you a thousand good reasons to come home to me. But you stole that from me. You wanted me happy? Well, guess what? You failed. For twelve fucking years I have been heartbroken, and sad, and so fucking lost without my best friend." After that gut shot, Lily didn't wait for my response. She turned and stomped away to the back of the hangar.

Wisely, Levi, Jasper, and Clark didn't say a word. All three busied themselves pretending like they had not witnessed that exchange.

I had made a mess of everything. She was right, I had stolen her happiness. I didn't have to fake my death, but we made that choice because of who my father was. At the time, I thought it was the right decision. Now, I realized how badly I had fucked up.

I needed to talk to her, make her understand why

I did what I did. I started to follow her when Clark stopped me.

"Give her a minute." I cut my eyes to the hand Clark had on my forearm. "Trust me, Lenox, give her some time to cool off. She's completely overwhelmed. You don't think I knew that earlier when I was grilling her? All that fake bravado was to cover up that she was scared shitless. When she masked her fears and offered to look at those pictures, it was so she wouldn't break down in front of us. She is a strong woman. I don't know how she was when you two were younger, but I suspect she was stronger than you recognized. Let her have this."

Damn if he wasn't right. She needed to cool off, and I still needed to figure out how Clyde Davidson played into Roman's plan.

The problem was we were trying to profile a complete lunatic, and that was not my area of expertise. We had analysts and profilers for that. I was simply the firepower, the one they sent out to execute the plan.

"Are you sure he didn't know about Lily?" Jasper asked.

"Shit man, at this point anything is possible. I have a photo of Lily I keep in my safe, but when we go out on a mission, I always tuck her in my vest. He could've looked through my shit and found it."

"We have to keep in mind this might have been a stroke of good luck on his part," Clark added.

"You really believe that? When was the last time something involving Roman happened by chance? That fucker is methodical, he was trained to be that way," I asked.

"There is a first time for everything. What I mean is, I don't want to get lost down a rabbit hole. Let's concentrate on finding him and taking him out." Clark started to stack the pictures of Lily.

"I think I found something," Levi said. "Lily said that Roman told her he was going green. There is only one island in the Exumas that has windmills powering the island. It was renamed to Last Chance Cay five years ago when it was purchased by a Guy Borough from Nova Scotia. But there is no record of a Guy Borough, but there is a city named Guysborough in Nova Scotia. The five-year time frame also coincides with Kincaid's involvement with the producer, Davidson."

"The wire transfers to McGrath Carter initiated from a Royal Bank and Trust. There is a branch in Nova Scotia."

I glanced over my shoulder to the door Lily had

gone through. It was killing me not going to her. I wanted to pull her into my arms and make her forget about the shitstorm that had become her life. I desperately wanted to grab her and run away with her; we could change our names and never be heard from again. But that dream was impossible, and I needed to get a lock on Roman. There was no time to coddle her and smooth hurt feelings. I had to stop thinking like Shane and slip back into the trained killer I had become.

The sooner Roman was eliminated the, sooner I could get Lily back to her life and out of mine. The longer she was around, the harder it would be to watch her walk away.

13

It had been hours since I stormed out of the main room of the hangar and into a makeshift bunk room. There was a worn-out cot with a coarse green blanket and a wooden chair in the corner. I picked the wrong room to storm off to. I was starving and cold and getting madder by the minute. The hard wood under my ass was making my leg fall asleep, and I was cursing Shane for bringing me here. I wanted to go home. No, scratch that, I never wanted to go there again. Someone had defiled my home and videotaped me there. A hotel, that is where I wanted to go. But I couldn't. I was stuck here in a dirty room with my *dead* ex-best friend down the hall.

I tried to rationalize everything Shane had told me. All his reasons for leaving. Logically I understood...kinda. But emotionally I didn't understand how he could've done that to me. He had to have known what his death would do to me. He took choices away from me, and I think that part was what I was most pissed about. He hadn't trusted me enough to tell me what he was doing.

The door creaked open, and Jasper appeared, looking sympathetic. I had embarrassed the shit out of myself out there. All the strength I had tried to show was washed away in one single outburst.

"Sorry to bother you Lily, but it's time to move," Jasper said.

"Move? Where am I going?"

My heart started to pound in my chest, and panic was quickly coming to the surface. As mad as I was, I wasn't ready to say goodbye to Shane yet.

"Not just you. All of us. We have to keep moving. Have you ever ridden in a helicopter?" He smiled.

"No," I answered. Now panic was setting in for a whole new reason. I had never been in a helicopter, and there was a reason for that. I wasn't fond of heights.

"Then you're in for a treat. We have an Agusta A109C, and she is a beauty. Come on, the guys are ready."

I patted my back pocket to make sure my cell phone was still in there. Not that it mattered much in here; I had no cell phone signal, and my battery was almost dead from playing Candy Crush. I would need to charge it and check in with Rebecca soon. I always took the day of Shane's death off, but if I didn't check in by tomorrow, she'd be worried.

A thousand thoughts raced through my mind. Would I be allowed to call Rebecca? Would I have to fake my death? Was someone still after me? I was afraid to ask Shane. Terrified really to bring any of this up and have him send me away.

I followed him back into the main room. All of the white boards were wiped clean, laptops were gone, the photographs that were once spread over the table were absent. They had completely cleaned the space. Three computer monitors remained on a makeshift desk, but there was no computer attached.

Jasper held open the door leading to another large hangar. I don't know how I missed the other bay. It was a little frightening that I was so tired and overwhelmed I wasn't paying attention to my surroundings.

"Wow, that's bigger than I thought," I commented on the size of the helicopter. It was shiny silver with black pin striping and details. Levi was pulling it out with a four-wheeler on to the tarmac in front of the huge open door.

"That's what she said," Jasper chuckled.

"You just couldn't help yourself, could you?" I joined him laughing.

"Sorry. I lost my manners years ago. We spend most of our time hot and sweaty in third world countries. Our sense of humor is that of children. When you're stuck somewhere miserable, any laugh will help. Even the most juvenile."

I fully turned to look at Jasper. He was a good-looking guy. Tall and well built by the looks of how he filled out the tan tee he wore. He looked war-hardened and lonely. I can't explain how someone looked lonely, but he did. Like he craved some sort of affection. I wondered if Shane had that look, too. In the hours I spent with him, I was too caught up in myself to really look at him. I was either losing my shit on him or begging him to fuck me. I wasn't even going to examine why or how that had happened. Not only had I never asked a man to have sex with me, I had certainly never done it with such vulgarity.

I didn't regret that it happened, I only regretted that it was in a car and I didn't get to properly explore his body. And by the way things looked now, I never would.

"She's all ready," Levi called out when he pulled the four-wheeler back in the hanger and shut off the engine.

"Where are we going anyway?" I asked.

"Big Bear," Clark answered as he walked up behind us. I looked around the cavernous space looking for Shane, but I couldn't find him. "He hit the head," he informed me.

"Big Bear? Why don't we just drive? It's only about two hours west by car."

It seemed overly wasteful flying a helicopter only a hundred miles.

"It's a matter of safety. We can be followed in a car," Clark explained.

I guess that made sense. What the hell did I know about someone following you? Nothing, that's what. I had been completely oblivious to someone following me and taking pictures of me for months. I needed to look at those pictures more closely and figure out for how long. Not that it mattered much, I suppose Clark was only humoring me when I suggested it earlier.

I wasn't the priority, catching that guy Roman was. I felt so stupid that I had been completely duped by Calvin Kincaid. Thank God I never accepted his invitation to dinner.

"Let's roll," Shane threw over his shoulder as he made his way to the helicopter.

His voice sent shivers through my body, I still couldn't believe he was alive. Never in my wildest dreams did I ever think I'd see him again.

Walking behind him gave me a perfect view of his nice firm ass. I couldn't help but stare. Even his walk was sexy, his long legs ate up the distance in powerful strides. His confidence and power shone in the way he strutted. I couldn't see his eyes, but I was sure they were scanning the area for threats. So damn hot. Wait, I was mad at him, I shouldn't be drooling over him. I should've been plotting how to maim him after all the grief he had caused.

All too soon the show was over, and Jasper was helping me into the helicopter. I had flown on many private planes. Hell, my ex-husband and father both owned one, but I had never seen the inside of a helicopter. I didn't know what I expected, but it wasn't plush cream-colored leather seats and a glossy wood trim package.

I ducked inside and took a window seat. Jasper, Clark, and Shane followed in behind me.

"Who's the pilot?" I asked.

"Levi," Shane answered when he took the seat next to me.

Oh, goody, he was speaking to me again.

"Levi? There's not a real pilot?"

"Sweetheart, Levi is the best pilot I know," Clark laughed and took the seat across from me, Jasper taking the one next to him.

I heard a low rumble coming from beside me. Sheesh, someone was grumpy. I was about to ask Shane what his problem was when Levi interrupted me.

"Engine one a go. Clear rotor," he yelled out the open window. I looked out but didn't see anyone.

"Habit. He always calls when he is starting the engines. If someone were out there it would be dangerous," Jasper explained. I nodded my head in understanding. "Put your headset on." He pointed to a headset hanging from the roof of the cabin.

I watched as the other guys put them on and followed suit. As soon as they were snug over my ears, the engine noise was gone and I could hear Levi clearly.

"Fuel pressure up."

I felt, rather than heard, the whining of the engine. The cabin started to vibrate as the rotor blades gained speed. I hated heights, but so far this was exciting.

"Test," Levi's voice rang out in my headset.

"Copy." Three voices came over next.

My body gently started rocking with the swooshing of the blades chopping through the air. They were winding faster and faster until it was a steady strum. I startled when the helicopter lifted off the ground and started making a steady ascent. Shane's hand went to my thigh and stopped my bouncing knee.

"We're good. Everything will be fine, promise," Shane tried to reassure me.

"Last time you said that you pushed me out of an airplane," I reminded him.

"For someone who is afraid of heights, you sure did love it."

Ha! I didn't love it. I was scared shitless the whole way down. Little did Shane know I had only agreed to jump with him when he explained I would be strapped to him for a tandem jump. I had my eyes closed all the way down and enjoyed the feel of him pressed against my back.

I continued to look out the window as we passed over the bland, brown desert. There was nothing fascinating to focus on, leaving me to my wandering thoughts.

How in the hell did I get here? Yesterday I was living my uninteresting life, one day bleeding into the next. And today two men tried to abduct me. I still hadn't thought about or processed that Shane had killed them both right in front of me. Yet another thing I should've been freaking out about, but I was completely numb to it. That seemed to be the theme of the day. Everything else paled in comparison to me finding out that Shane was alive.

I suppose I should've started calling him Lenox or Carter or whatever the hell new name he was going to take once he left me again. A few hours ago, I thought I'd have the chance to convince him not to leave again, or to take me with him. But that was before I met Lenox. Lenox was nothing like Shane. He had changed so much over the years. I'd heard stories of men coming back from war completely different than when they left, but I'd never seen it firsthand.

Now that I had, and I had seen this new person in front of me, I wasn't sure I had a chance. Hell, I was still so pissed at him I wasn't sure I even wanted to stay with him. Who the hell was I kidding? Of course I wanted to stay with him. It didn't matter how mad I was or how bad he had hurt me. Those feelings would dissipate and leave me wanting him. Again.

"Ten minutes out," Levi said.

I blinked my eyes and focused on the ground, the desert had given way to evergreen trees and mountains. I had spaced out the entire ride.

"Where are we staying in Big Bear?" I asked.

There were plenty of hotels and resorts around the area, but being a tourist town, they were normally booked. Not to mention where the hell do you leave a helicopter?

"Lenox's place," Jasper answered.

"I'm sorry, I think I heard you wrong. Did you say Lenox's place? As in Shane?"

"Yes. We're gonna stay at my house," Shane answered.

Steam must've been coming out of my ears. He had a fucking house in Big Bear, two hours from where I lived. Not to mention, Big Bear was one of my two favorite spots to drive to when I needed to relax.

"Nice," I snickered. "Next thing you're gonna tell me you own a house in Monterey, too."

Jerk.

He didn't answer nor did he look at me. He did - he had a house there, too. Un-fucking-real.

"Why? Why would you buy real estate in those places? Are you trying to torture me?"

"Not now." He tightened his grip on my thigh.

Damn, I had forgotten he had put his hand there. I quickly swiped it off and crossed my arms over my chest. I could feel my tears starting to swim in my lids and prayed they wouldn't fall. I couldn't cry in front of these men. I need to put my "Lillian Nelson" armor on and be the ice queen my father had taught me to be. My only problem was, I'd never been able to be her around Shane.

A beautiful log cabin came into view. It was more of a chalet than a regular cabin. It was huge with a large clearing around the house. But the property was surrounded by trees.

"Is that Bluffs Lodge?" I asked.

We had camped there many times when we were in high school.

"It is," Shane confirmed.

"And you bought a house near Bluffs Lodge?" I questioned him.

"It was your favorite place up here," he stated. As if that answered my question.

Levi landed the helicopter in front of Shane's massive home with ease. Or maybe he didn't. I was so preoccupied planning ways to strangle a Ranger... black ops...badass - whatever the hell he was - to notice how we actually made it to the ground.

The guys all moved around taking off their headsets, opening the cabin doors, talking to one another while I stayed frozen in my seat. The vibrations started to lessen, and the slicing of the blades slowed and finally came to a stop. I saw Clark's lips moving and his hand gesturing for me to get out, but I was still in a state of disbelief and unable to make myself come unglued. The shock was too much.

Why? Shane had gone to such great lengths to extradite me from his life, why did he continue to insinuate himself into mine?

Clark continued to stare at me, his eyes softening in understanding. With a sad smile, he nodded his head and tapped Jasper on the shoulder, leaving Shane there to deal with me.

"Lily," he whispered.

That was all it took for the tears I was fighting to fall.

14

There were no words for the pain I felt at that moment. My carefully ordered world had come crashing down on me. Lily was shattered, and it was all my doing. She was slowly learning how deep my betrayal went, how close I was to her all these years without her ever knowing.

"I want to go back to yesterday when I didn't know...didn't know you were alive. That pain was easier than this," she cried.

I jumped back into the helicopter and pulled her onto my lap, letting her sob into my chest. She felt so good in my arms, even her tears felt right. She was where she belonged. Where she should've always been.

"Why?" she asked.

There was no easy answer to that question. Nothing I could explain would ease her pain.

"Because I am a selfish prick. Because when my world was dark, I needed some of your light. Something that made me feel clean and good. Anything to give me just a sliver of you." I brushed her hair from her face so I could see her pretty eyes. They were shiny with unshed tears. She was so damn beautiful it made my heart ache. "You loved it up here. I have memories of us here, camping and waterskiing at the lake, you sunbathing on the shore. I could come here and feel close to you, to us. When I go to Monterey, I can sit on the pier and watch the seals playing in the water and remember your smile. I needed something to hold on to. If I couldn't have you, I needed the *memory* of you."

And that was the God's honest truth. I needed her. I would've completely lost myself if I didn't have her to ground me. All the bad shit I've seen, all the horrific things I've had to do in the name of God and Country, she is what kept me sane.

We sat there for long moments in silence, both of us lost in our own thoughts. I couldn't bring myself to insult her by saying I was sorry. They would've been empty words. I wasn't sorry I faked my death to keep her safe. I was sorry, however, for the aftermath, all the agony and grief I caused. But in the years I was away, she had found herself. Lily was an amazing woman and had pulled herself up and created something good. If she had stayed with me, that would've never happened.

"Come on babe, let's get you inside. I need to feed you, and we need to figure out what to do about Rebecca."

She didn't speak but acknowledged me with a nod of her head.

We exited the helicopter, and I caught Levi in my peripheral vision. He was far enough away not to hear our conversation but still close enough to have my six. I didn't know what I'd do without my team. The three of them are like my brothers; we were thick as thieves and always have each other's backs. The four of us made the perfect team.

Could I walk away from them? My gut knotted at the mere thought of leaving the Army, but my heart tightened just as painfully when I thought about not having Lily. Was it even possible for me to leave with her and live some normal life? Was I mentally equipped to work at a hardware store somewhere selling tools? Could I leave my brothers and pretend to be a regular Joe off the street and not a trained killer? I didn't see how I could possibly do that. And I couldn't keep Lily while I was off trying to save the world, either. I was in a lose-lose situation. Bottom line, I was fucked.

As soon as we walked in the door, I heard Clark and Jasper in the kitchen banging around. Trying to find food no doubt, and beer. They were definitely trying to find the alcohol.

"Man, you got nothin' in this place," Clark yelled.

Lily stood by my side stock still, her eyes taking in the vaulted ceilings and large windows. The cabin was rustic and done in deep browns and reds. There were no personal effects downstairs in the main room. It was completely generic and lifeless.

There was one thing I needed to show her, and I might as well get it over with now.

"Cases of beer are in the garage. There should be steaks and burgers in the freezer. I'm taking Lily upstairs to get cleaned up. If you need anything else take the Yukon to town and buy something," I yelled back, directing Lily toward the stairs.

She still hadn't uttered a word. This was so different than the Lily I knew. When she was pissed, she yelled. When you made her really mad, you got the hot side of her tongue and she'd cut you down to size. And if she was happy, the whole world lit up with her joy. It was a beautiful thing. Everyone gravitated to her in high school. I know she thought it was because of her family name, and for some, that was the reason. But for others, they just wanted a piece of her happiness. This silence was a new thing, and it worried me. I wanted her to rage and yell. She needed to process everything that had happened, not shut down.

We made our way upstairs and through the open loft that looked over the downstairs, coming to a stop in front of my bedroom door. I debated whether or not to warn her, but what was I going to say, *hey Lily I swung by my parent's house and took all of my personal belongings out of my room*? I didn't think there was a way to tell her, so I simply opened the door and allowed her to see for herself.

"Oh my God." She covered her mouth with her hands as she took in the room.

My football trophies and state championship medals were displayed on a side table. The comforter draped over the bed was the one I had in high school. I even had the framed Rocky Horror Picture Show original movie poster hung on the wall that Lily had given me for my seventeenth birthday.

We used to sneak out to the Valley and see the midnight showing. We both knew all the lines.

Those nights were some of the best nights. Every time I looked at the poster, I could picture Lily singing and dancing in the aisle of the theater.

It might've sounded ridiculous for a grown man to have replicated his childhood bedroom complete with trophies, but this was all I had left of her. She had been present and cheering me on when I earned each of those awards. That was the comforter she would wrap herself up in when she would lay on my bed. She had slept curled up in that very blanket many times. I couldn't bear to part with any of it.

I stood in the doorway while she walked to the bed and ran her hand over the cover. She remembered, too. Many nights we slept together in my bed. She and I talking into the early morning hours before we both passed out next to each other. Never a single kiss between us, not an inappropriate touch or fondle. Just two best friends enjoying each other.

Even when she had a boyfriend, or I was seeing some girl, she would still stay the night. I know no one in high school believed we weren't sleeping together. Our friendship caused a lot of problems in her dating life. It was never an issue for me, I didn't have girlfriends. There were plenty of girls I fucked but never on the bed I shared with Lily and never anyone that could compare to her.

She crawled into the bed and pulled the comforter up to her face, cuddling into it. Chills ran over my body as I watched her. I was transported back to another time and place. One of innocence and naïveté. Her being in my bed represented all that I had wanted and all that I had given up. Years. I'd spent years imagining her in my bed again. Only this time I wouldn't've been noble. I would've been the one to take her virginity, not hear about some fumbling idiot who barely knew what he was doing. I would've taken my time with her and showed her what it meant to make love.

I would've told her how I felt, how much I loved her. How much I hated to hear about her dates because it should've been me. I would've grown a pair of balls and claimed what was mine.

But I was a pussy and too afraid I would turn into my parents and hurt her. I knew she deserved better than me.

The sound of her crying pulled me from my reverie. I went to the bed and got in beside her, pulling her onto my chest.

I wished she would scream at me again. I could take her anger, but her tears were cutting me to the quick. I was powerless to stop her sadness. I did the only thing I could do and held her tight, stroking her back trying to soothe some of the hurt.

"Lily, I don't know what to do to help you," I admitted.

She held on to me, and slowly her sobs turned into soft hiccups. Her hand that was on my chest started to move. Slowly at first, tentative light touches. She maneuvered her hand under my shirt and sparks shot through my body.

I could feel.

Her small hand glided over the ridges and valleys of my abs and up to my pecs. She stopped to run her fingers over the charm that once belonged to her then back down to the waistband of my jeans.

"Make it go away," she whispered.

"How Lily?"

Her soft fingertips continued to brush my bare skin. My body was on fire with a lust that solely belonged to her.

"I don't want to feel or think. I need you to take it all away."

She sat up and pulled her shirt over her head and tossed it away. The pink lacy bra was next, exposing her tits. The next few moments were a frenzy of motion as we both divested ourselves of our clothes.

I didn't need her to ask me again as I rolled her

under me. My hand went to her pussy, feeling the wetness that awaited me. I pushed two fingers inside of her and her back arched. Stunning. I worked her up with my fingers until I felt her inner muscles start to tighten. I didn't want her to come on my fingers, I needed her to wait until I was buried inside of her and we both let go together.

She started to protest when she lost my fingers, but the words quickly died on her lips when in one steady thrust I was balls deep inside of her.

"Shane," she groaned.

That single word was almost my undoing. My name spilling from her lips while I was inside of her did crazy things to my heart. I took her mouth in a soul-scorching kiss. This kiss was going to make me or break me. Either I would take the memory of this kiss with me and it would sustain me over the years, or I would crumble under the weight of it.

I set a bruising pace as I drove into her with all the built-up need and love I had for her.

"I need you to feel, Lily." I kissed down her face to the crook of her neck. "I need you to feel every inch of me inside of you. My body covering yours. How much I love you."

"I love you, Shane," she moaned.

"Only you, Lily, it's always been you," I admitted.

"I never want to forget this moment," she whispered.

"You won't. I'll make sure of it."

I slowed my pace, giving her long lazy strokes drawing out our pleasure. Each time I felt her pussy start to spasm, I stopped and languidly kissed her until the feeling subsided. Then working us both back into a fever, only to stop again.

With her body trembling under mine, I finally let go, pushing us both over the edge. Both of us cried out in pleasure as I released into her. Long after we both orgasmed, I stayed inside of her kissing her throat, face, and lips. Anywhere I could reach without pulling out. I didn't want this feeling to end.

Soon the glazed look of passion faded from her eyes, and she breathed out a content sleepy sigh.

I rolled off of Lily and situated her back to my front, hugging her to me.

We laid in bed for hours drifting in and out of sleep, making love again and again. A smile tugged at my lips when I pushed out of bed remembering how Lily looked when I took her from behind, her tits swaying from my hard thrusts. She would definitely be sore tomorrow. I took her hard and rough and in as many positions as I could. I needed to get my fill; I didn't know when she'd be taken from me again.

There was a constant nagging feeling in my gut. I knew this was a mistake, I knew that we'd both be devastated when she had to leave. But I couldn't help myself. She was my obsession.

I tagged my clothes off the floor and quickly dressed, with one last long look I left a naked sleeping Lily in my bed. What I wouldn't give to have that for a lifetime.

When I got downstairs, the guys were sitting on the back deck playing cards, all with beers in their hands. I had to chuckle to myself when I saw the unopened bottle of whiskey on the table. None of them would take a sip of liquor while they were on watch. Beer was okay, but the hard stuff was off-limits. As safe as we were here, they'd never take the chance of being drunk if someone were to find us.

"About fucking time, lover boy," Levi commented when I opened the back door.

The cool, crisp air hit me, and I inhaled the fresh pine scent of the mountains. I loved the way it smelled up here - clean, untouched by smog and pollution.

"Fuck off. Did you save me any?" I nodded toward the empty plates on the table.

"Yeah, we saved your sorry ass some. You're lucky too 'cause Levi grills up a mean fuckin' T-bone," Jasper laughed.

I *was* lucky, the bunch of them were fucking animals, they could eat a whole damn cow. I found two steaks covered with foil in the kitchen. Baked potatoes and green beans next to that. Damn these assholes went all out, no doubt it was to impress Lily. If it had just been us up here, they would've brought back a pizza.

After I fixed a plate, I went back out on the deck to relax with the guys. The moment I sat down everyone's demeanor changed.

"You had your fill?" Clark asked taking a long pull from his beer.

"Come again," I growled. I prayed to God he wasn't implying what I thought he was.

"Lily. You had your fill of her yet? You were up there drilling her ass the last four hours," Clark continued.

I had to take a deep breath to calm myself down. I normally wasn't a hothead. In fact, I was known for being the cold, methodical one. But right now, my friend was pushing me to a point I was afraid we'd never come back from.

"Man, I love you like a brother. But if you ever

refer to Lily as a piece of ass again, I will gut you. And I hope to say this only once, because if I have to say it again, it will be the end of our friendship. Lily is not some skanky barfly we pick up and bang for the night and compare stories about the next day. That woman upstairs is my world, and you will treat her with the respect she deserves."

I leaned over my steak and cut into it, not sparing a look at my team. I was so fucking angry I couldn't even taste the first bite as I chewed.

"Good to know, brother. I wanted to make sure she was who I thought she was," Clark replied.

"And who did you think she was?" I asked abandoning my food.

"The game changer." Clark eyed me as I took in his words.

"What the fuck are you talking about?"

The man had finally lost his ever-loving mind. What the fuck, did he think this was some hearts and flowers fairy tale? Just because I spent hours making love to the woman didn't mean a damn thing had changed.

"I mean the one thing that can take you out of the game. Change your life and put everything into perspective."

Oh yeah, he definitely thought this was a Hollywood drama come to life.

"I'm squared away, man. I have my eye on the prize."

I didn't, I was lying through my teeth, but they didn't need to know that.

"Really? So no regrets? You wouldn't give this all up for the love of that woman upstairs?" Clark asked.

"Nope. Regrets are for the Air Force, I'm a Ranger," I replied.

"You're a fucking liar is what you are. And I wouldn't be a friend if I didn't warn you against making a mistake you'll beat yourself up about for the rest of your life."

I know there was a woman in Clark's past. That was obviously clouding his better judgment at the moment.

"Noted." I picked up the bottle of whiskey, cracked the seal, and unscrewed the lid. All the while thinking about my many regrets. When I put the bottle to my lips and took the first pull, I started to formulate a plan. As the whiskey burned down my throat, I hated myself for what I was about to do.

15

It had been a glorious week. Dare I say it, the best week of my entire life. I called Rebecca and asked her if she would watch over the centers for me, that I was going to finally take that vacation she had been nagging me about. She was thrilled for me and told me to take as much time as I needed, she'd handle everything. There was a slight twinge of guilt as the lie slipped past my lips. But Shane quickly reminded me that the lie was necessary to protect her and my centers.

We spent our days hiking on the alpine trails, Shane taught me how to shoot, and we all hung out together playing cards and drinking whiskey. Shane was a good sport when the guys busted his chops about me being a card shark. Secretly, I think he loved I could beat them all at poker. Shane had taught me how to play when we were younger.

He did mumble under his breath about shooting Levi if he ever suggested strip poker again. The guys all treated me like I was their long-lost sister. Once Clark warmed up to me and started acting like himself, I figured him for the leader of the group. Levi was very thoughtful, a deep thinker, and seemed very reserved. Jasper was a riot, always cracking jokes and being the funny one, but you could tell he was deeply wounded. As much as he fooled around, you could tell he was overcompensating for something. I didn't know what, and he'd never tell me, but it was there in his soulful eyes.

There had been no more talk of the past or the future or what was going to happen. It was like there was an unspoken moratorium. We were going to enjoy whatever time we had together. I knew I was being a fool, but I couldn't help falling more in love with Shane. Losing the innocent teenage love I had for him was the hardest thing I ever had to go through. Losing him now would kill me. I was taking a huge risk, one I couldn't begin to control or stop. I had no defenses against him. There was zero way to stop my heart as it fused with his. He owned me, and as scared as I was, it was exciting and exhilarating. I didn't want this feeling to ever end. More than ever I was willing to fight for him.

It was the afternoon of the eighth day at the cabin when Clark's cell phone rang as we walked into the house.

"I'm gonna go shower." I kissed Shane's cheek and headed for the stairs.

I made my way to Shane's room and rushed through my shower. I wanted to hurry and start dinner. We had stopped on our way home from the lake and picked up fresh vegetables to grill with the trout we caught today.

I was wrapping myself up in a towel when Shane stepped into the bedroom.

"Hey, did Levi start the grill?" I asked. "I'll be down in a jiff." I finished drying off and dropped the towel, pulling on a pair of fresh panties. Shane watched silently from the doorway. "Everything alright?"

I stopped fidgeting with my bra and gave him my full attention. The look on his face told me everything I needed to know. Intuitively my eyes drifted close and fury hit my belly.

"It's time?" I asked.

"Yes," he replied. His voice was completely devoid of any emotion.

I don't know what panicked me more, the uncertainty of what was about to happen or the cold hard expression Shane wore.

This man standing in front of me was not my Shane, he had Lenox firmly in place.

"We've already called in the standby team. Peter and James will be here in thirty minutes," Shane informed me.

"Thirty minutes?" I screeched, and the tears that were threatening, started to spill down my cheeks. "When will you be back?"

"I won't."

"You won't? What does that mean? When will I see you?" I asked.

My mind was racing, and I tried to fight off the feeling of déjà vu but I couldn't. In my mind, I was transported back to the hotel room when Shane told me he was leaving on deployment. The words and circumstances were different, but the feeling was the same.

"You won't. In a few days, you'll go back to your life, and I will be gone again."

"No," I cried.

My heart was shattering into a million pieces and he was so nonchalant he might as well have been talking about the weather. I tried to find some sort of emotion in his eyes, anything that would tell me he was hurting as badly as me. But there was nothing there. Absolutely nothing.

"Lily." His tone was abrupt and harsh.

"You are not doing this again Shane. I won't let you leave me." I tried my hardest to sound brave and confident. I needed to fight for us, fight for him. I had to stay strong.

"You don't have a choice. Nothing has changed, Lillian."

Lillian? The use of my full name set me off. He sounded like he was scolding an unruly child who wouldn't fall in line.

"Don't *Lillian* me. Everything has changed. You admitted you loved me. We just spent seven days together, making love. Are you telling me that meant nothing?"

"It meant nothing to me. I thought that I could find a piece of the old me in you. Remember how my life was before I joined the 707. I thought there was a possibility that I may've wanted that life again. I was wrong. The only thing the last seven days taught me is you can't go back in time. The feelings that I had for you aren't real. They're gone. I am not that starry-eyed little boy anymore. I'm sorry, but I don't love you like that."

His words were like a torpedo to my soul. Each and every one of them tore me to shreds. When I gained the courage to look him in the eye, I was shocked to find hurt.

"You're a fucking liar. You think I don't know you. You think I don't know everything you just said was complete bullshit? You're a coward, Shane Owings. You were twelve years ago, and you still are. You're too afraid to reach out and grab what's right in front of you. You look me in the eye and tell me the last week has meant nothing, that us making love was meaningless to you."

I held his eyes and locked my legs to stop them from shaking. My emotions were so frazzled I couldn't even find the strength to put on the Lillian Nelson Ice Queen façade.

"Do you know how many women I have fucked over the last decade? Hundreds, maybe even thousands. I have had a new woman in every country after every mission, sometimes more than one if the first didn't burn through the frustration."

That was a direct shot to my heart, and that information ripped through me, as well.

"Tell me you don't love me," I demanded.

"Just a few weeks ago this cute little thing

Stephanie or Sarah or something had the pleasure of gracing my bed," he continued.

"I don't give a rat's rear end who you've slept with or when. You're deflecting, Shane. Tell me you don't love me," I screamed.

"I don't love you," he spat out.

"You're a fucking coward and a liar." He was lying. He had to be. There was no way this was one-sided. "You wanna know how I know you're full of shit? Because when your hands are touching me, your eyes catch fire. When you pull away after kissing me, you have a smile on your face. When your eyes meet mine after we make love, you are at peace. I can see it, I can feel it, and most of all *you* feel it, too. We are one, Shane. We always have been."

"What do you want from me? I told you what you wanted to hear, I don't love you. This meant nothing. It was a way to finally get you out of my system. Now that it's done, it's time to move on. I have another mission to get ready for, and you have a life to live."

"That's it. You leave, I never see you again?" I asked.

"Yes."

"Please don't do this, Shane. I love you. I can't lose you again," I begged.

"This is the right thing to do. You don't know me, not anymore. I'm not the man you think I am. I will only hurt and disappoint you. You're better off without me in your life. Don't visit that grave anymore. As much as that man is dead and gone, he doesn't deserve your pain or loyalty. Move on with your life and be happy." Shane stopped at the bedroom door. "You deserve to be happy, Lily. Forget you ever knew me. Goodbye."

With those words, he left me standing in his bedroom broken.

I crawled into the bed that still smelled like him and sobbed. I didn't go after him like I had promised myself I would. Hearing him say goodbye was too much for me to take. I knew he was lying to himself and to me when he said the last week meant nothing to him. But I wasn't strong enough to fight Lenox.

I cried myself to sleep and had no idea when the guys left, or when the new guys got to the house to babysit me. The moment my eyes opened I regretted not going downstairs to say goodbye to Levi, Jasper, and Clark. After the rocky start I had with Clark, he proved to be a good man and friend. I would miss the three of them.

"Ms. Nelson?" I heard my name being called from the other side of the door and the accompanying knock.

The unfamiliar voice startled me and I contemplated not answering, but I was afraid they would come in and I was still only in my bra and panties.

"Just a minute," I answered. I glanced around the room momentarily disoriented in the near darkness.

Finding my dirty clothes in a pile on the floor, I made quick work of getting dressed. I didn't bother fixing my hair, even though it looked like a rat had nested in it. There was no one I was trying to impress.

"Yes?" I asked when I opened the door.

"Lenox said that you had not eaten. I wanted to see if you were ready for supper?" the man asked, his Texas drawl distinguishable now that there was not a closed door separating us.

"And you are?" I inquired.

"Sorry, ma'am, I'm Peter," he introduced himself.

"Nice to meet you, Peter. I'm sorry for all the trouble babysitting me may have caused you. Thank you for the offer of supper, but I'm not hungry."

Peter was a good-looking man. Maybe that was a prerequisite for joining the 707. God knows Shane was sexy as hell, and Levi, Jasper, and Clark were all pretty hot too.

"Lenox said I was to make sure you ate tonight," Peter informed me.

"Is that so? Well luckily for us Lenox is long gone. He'll never know," I snapped. It wasn't Peter's fault that Shane was an asshole. The poor guy didn't deserve my bad attitude. "Sorry, that was rude. Thank you for your concern, but I'm really not hungry right now."

"Not even for pizza? Pepperoni and mushroom?" Peter asked.

"Asshole," I whispered.

"Ma'am?"

"Sorry, not you, you're not the asshole. Lenox is. In one breath, he shatters me then his actions show he cares." Peter was staring at me confused. "Pepperoni and mushroom is my favorite. When we were kids, anytime I was upset he always came over with a pizza. He hates mushrooms but still ate them just because I liked them." I had no business spilling my guts to this guy. "Anyway, you don't care about my woes. I'll let you get back to whatever it is you guys do. I won't be any trouble. I'll stay in my room."

"I'm a good listener, we could share a pizza and a beer. You can talk or not - whatever you need."

I took a minute to study Peter and contemplated his offer for a second. He had a genuine easy way about him. I didn't want to talk about Shane, but getting out of the room I shared with him was probably a good idea.

I looked back at the bed and thought about stripping the sheets down and washing them, but I wasn't ready for that just yet. I needed to be close to him for one more night.

"You know what? I'll take you up on the pizza and beer."

Before I left the bedroom, I stepped in front of the dresser to check my appearance in the mirror. That's when I noticed it. My necklace. The one Shane had taken all those years ago. The one he said he never took off. I sucked in an excruciating breath as I felt my heart truly break and leave my chest.

He was really gone.

16

Hot searing pain ripped through my shoulder. Before I had time to get a shot off, I heard Levi's voice crackle in my ear. "Fall back. You have two unfriendlies at your three o'clock."

"Fuck," Clark hissed. "Lenox, you pull some stupid shit like that again and I will yank your ass off this op so fast your fucked-up head will spin."

"Someone needed to draw them out. A graze to the shoulder is a small price," I answered.

But damn it still hurt. It had been a long time since I'd been shot - I forgot how painful it could be. Clark didn't have anything further to say, he knew I was right. We needed to draw out the shooters before we could make our way into the house. They had the advantage of higher ground; if we charged the house they could pick us off.

"Cover, ground team. Frag out," Levi instructed.

We took cover behind a sorry ass excuse of a tiki bar as the grenade Levi fired took out the side of the building the two men were firing from. I had never been so thankful for shoddy Bahamian construction.

"Tango down," Levi called in. "Charlie Mike."

"Roger," Clark confirmed the order to continue the mission.

Clark and Jasper both had their dive boots off and Solomons out of the dry pack before I had my first wet boot pulled off. I winced as the salt water, sweat, and sand abraded the bullet graze. Fuck, we did not have time for this.

"Get a hop on it, Lenox," Jasper said, adjusting his vest and covering us as I continued to struggle with my shoes.

I hated the beach, sand was a bitch to maneuver in. Coming in on the sea side of the cay was our only option for cover. The rock formations and thick foliage gave us someplace to hide as Levi made his way on the beach to our far left. He had a steep rock face to climb, but it was the perfect place for him to perch as our over watch.

With my dry boots on we were ready to hike to the other side of the cay where the main house was located. The latest intel put Roman on the island. His seaplane had been seen landing two days ago. The local government was of no help, they were easily bought. Luckily for us, the locals were too. The fish and game warden was a nosy bastard; he made it his business to be in the know. Not much went on in the wildlife park where Roman's cay was situated in without the warden's notice. He was on the take too - the man had no loyalties, the information he had sold to the highest bidder.

We spent the last three weeks chasing our tails. The first report that had Roman in Cozumel was a bust. By the time we made it there, he was gone. We were greeted, however, by his entire household staff executed and a message for our team. The note simply read, "one step ahead."

Roman was getting desperate. He knew we were closing in and he had two options left - stand and fight or close his operation and go to ground. Knowing Roman the way we did, we knew there wasn't a chance he'd run and hide. He was preparing for his final stand. This was his end game, where he thought he would finally take us out. Arrogant prick thought he had one up on us, but little did he know that I no longer had anything to lose. I was just as dangerous as him.

Lily was gone. I'd made sure of it. I was the cold methodical asshole I was trained to be and cut her heart out with surgical precision. I needed her to hate me so she would never look back, and move on and live her life. There was no doubt I had succeeded. I watched the shine dim from her eyes when I said goodbye. She understood the finality in those words - I would never see her again. It was better this way. She was better off seeing the real me, the man I had become, rather than carry with her some false perception of goodness. I was not the teenage boy she once loved. I was a soulless killer. That's what I was taught to be and that is all I'll ever be. I took an oath to protect my country to the detriment of myself, and I fully intended to keep that oath.

More shots rang out, and I mechanically returned fire. Four more of Roman's men lay dead in the sand. This is what I was good at. Killing the enemy, not hearts and rainbows.

"Anyone think it's strange that there is not more security on the cay?" I asked.

"I've counted twelve so far," Jasper answered.

"Something smells bad. Watch your six boys, this is a set-up," Clark added.

With Jasper to my left and Clark to my right, we breached the front door of the main house. The moment we entered my world came to a crashing halt.

Lily.

How the fuck had Roman gotten to her? She was supposed to be safely tucked away in Big Bear with Peter and James.

17

Lily – Two days earlier

For three weeks, I had been locked up in this cabin. I was officially bored. Peter had been great about keeping me occupied, but there was only so much a person could do in the house. I wasn't allowed to go outside, so no more hiking, fishing, or trips to the store. James was standoffish and quiet. He barely spoke to me and was even short with Peter. No amount of reassurance on Peter's part made me comfortable around James. I was actively trying to avoid him. I didn't like the way he looked at me, like I was a bother. As much as I tried not to take it personally, I'm sure the last thing he wanted to be doing was babysitting, but his attitude was starting to piss me off.

I had just stepped into the sunroom when I heard the front door slam. "Lily. The safe room, now," Peter shouted.

The glass of iced tea I was holding slipped from my hand and shattered on the tile floor. The cool liquid and ice hit my feet, shocking me into motion. But before I could move more than a few feet, Peter's body jerked forward and he fell to the floor. James was right behind him with the proverbial smoking gun in his hand.

"I wouldn't bother, sweetheart, your ride is here," James sneered now, pointing the gun at me.

I had nowhere to go, Peter was too far away from me to try and get his gun now laying on the floor near his bleeding body. James was standing between me and any exits.

"Thanks, James, I've got it from here." Calvin Kincaid's smooth voice came from the doorway.

How was this possible? Shane and the team were out tracking Roman.

"Anytime, Roman," James replied.

"You traitorous asshole," I yelled.

"That's funny coming from you of all people. You've done nothing but mope around this house and cry over a man that clearly doesn't want you.

You should be happy that Roman will make him suffer for what he's done to you," James said.

I shook my head in disgust. "You'll rot in hell for this. Wait until I tell the guys what you've done. They'll hunt you down like the dog you are and kill you."

"That's sweet you think the team will be alive to do anything," James laughed.

"How could you?" I asked.

This didn't make any sense. James was a trusted member of Shane's team.

"How could I? You really are a naïve twit. You of all people should understand; loyalty has a price. Do you know how many years I've put my ass on the line for the 707? Three more years than that dumbfuck, Clark. Yet, I am passed over for Command Sergeant Major and Clark slides into the promotion that should've been mine. Fuck him, fuck the team, and fuck the 707. I'm looking out for me from now on. Roman simply had a better job offer and a pay raise," James sneered.

"Job offer! You sold out your team because you didn't get a promotion and money?"

There was no time for James to answer me, he continued to laugh until Calvin Kincaid shot him in the back of the head. There was no warning, no preamble; he simply raised his gun and shot him.

"I can't believe you did that," I shouted. "You killed him. Right in front of me."

"Yes, dear, I did. He was annoying and his usefulness ran out." Calvin shrugged his shoulders like it was all in a day's work. Completely unaffected that he had killed someone. "Come. We have places to be."

"I'm not going with you." I stepped back trying to put distance between us.

"Sure you will. Because you are the only person keeping Shane Owings alive. I left a trail for him to find me, he needs to see you at the end of the path for my plan to work."

"Well, Calvin, the joke is on you. Shane made it very clear I mean nothing to him. So, your plan isn't worth a shit. You'll need to find something else," I explained.

Admitting that hurt, but it was the truth. Shane left, and in the three weeks he's been gone, he stayed true to his word and hadn't contacted me. I didn't even know if he had been in contact with Peter.

"Women are so stupid. You really believe that Lenox hid you and protected you for twelve years, visited that stupid gravesite every year so he could see you, only to come back to command and drink himself into a stupor after every visit because you're meaningless?" Calvin threw his head back and chuckled. "Well then, I guess we'll go to plan B. I'll have to appeal to the mother in you."

"Excuse me?" I asked.

My hurt and anger toward Shane had now firmly slid into overwhelming fear. I shoved my hands into the pockets of my shorts in an effort to hide how badly I was shaking.

"You heard me, Mommy. Either you come with me now or I can let you walk out that door. But know that if you leave, you'll spend the rest of your life waiting for me to show back up. And when I do, I'll take that baby you're growing in your belly. You never know what I'll do. I could be nice and kill it right then and there in front of you, or I might just take it, leaving you to wonder what I did with it."

"You're a sick freak," I yelled, instinctively covering my belly with my hands.

"Not a freak. I am simply a man who knows how to get what I want. Come, we've wasted enough time here."

"And what do you want?" I asked.

Calvin cocked his head to the side and studied me for a minute before he answered, "I suppose I want what everyone wants - wealth and power. And unfortunately for you, you're my ticket to both."

"I have money. I'll give you whatever you want."

If money was what he was after that was easy, I had millions. I would gladly hand every last cent over to him if it meant that Shane's team and my baby would be safe.

"That would be too easy, sweetheart. I like to earn my money. Besides, it's going to be entertaining to watch Lenox when he sees you. I've been waiting to see the look of fear and panic cross his face for years. Ever since I first heard about you, actually. I never liked the smug prick. Rich boy trying to play soldier." Roman stopped, a look of disgust crossing his face. "All because mommy and daddy were mean to him," he mocked. "He really should be more careful when he's drunk. Lovesick fool spilled his guts after he saw you at the cemetery. I kept the whisky flowing, and by the end of the night I knew the whole story. How he met you, his academy award winning father, his whore of a mother. She's a good fuck by the way. I made sure to seek her out after I finally found you."

Shane was going to come completely unhinged when he found out that he told Roman everything he needed to know to find me. The guilt would be crippling, and I was afraid what Shane would do when Roman dropped the bomb. And he would, Roman was going to rub it in Shane's face while he sat back and watched the shit show that would follow.

"Storytime is over, Lillian. It's time to get the show on the road."

Calvin didn't wait for my answer, the smug bastard walked out the door knowing I'd follow. Of my own accord, I climbed in the back of the waiting SUV. I would rather go with him now at peace in the knowledge I was going to die along with my unborn child than walk this earth knowing that one day he'd be back to kill the life I was growing.

"How'd you know?" I asked once we were settled in the car.

"Peter told James he was going out to get you a pregnancy test. You know you really should be more careful who you tell your secrets to," Calvin answered, a wide smile on his face. "It really is a shame you'll have to raise the baby on your own. I hear being a single mother is difficult. You could always stay with me and I can play daddy."

"I'd rather die," I spat out. The thought of being anywhere around this man made me want to vomit.

"That can be arranged, Lily."

18

Lenox - Present day

Seeing Lily in the hands of a madman was my worst fear come true. Terror pumped through my veins and I had to force myself to remain calm. If anything happened to her I was as good as dead. I couldn't imagine a world without Lily's bright smile shining. All my years of suffering were in vain; here she was caught up again in a shitstorm of my doing.

I didn't have time to contemplate how Roman had found her, or where James and Peter were. I had to focus if I wanted to get Lily out of here alive. But there would be hell to pay when we left this island. How the fuck had we not known that Lily was here? We would never have stormed the cay if we had known Roman had her. The plan of attack would've been very different; without proper intel we had inadvertently put Lily in grave danger.

"How nice of you to finally join us. I was wondering what was taking so long," Roman laughed. "I guess the good 'ol US of A is slacking on their intel these days. Good to know."

"Let her go, Roman. It's me you want, she has nothing to do with this." I cut right to the chase.

I did a quick body scan of Lily. She was tied to a chair; her cheek was bruised, but other than that, I couldn't see any blood or obvious signs of injury.

Roman went about untying Lily from the chair, pulling her to stand in front of him, using her as a shield. Fucking cowardice dick.

"You think I want you, Lenox? I will admit it is mildly amusing seeing the constipated look on your face now that you know I have your girlfriend. But not nearly as satisfying as I thought it would be," Roman continued to laugh. "Let's stop wasting time and get down to brass tacks boys. How bad do you want Lillian?"

"Let Lily go. We are all here, let's settle this like men," Clark interjected.

"Settle this? I have nothing to settle with you," Roman replied.

"She has nothing to do with this." I tried to keep

my temper in check, but the longer his hands were on my woman, the harder it became. I dared not look at Lily, too afraid that if I saw the fear in her eyes I would lose the battle and detonate.

"Do with this? Have you poor assholes been chasing my tail around the globe thinking I was holding a grudge? Jesus Christ, you all really are idiots. Money, boys. Good old-fashioned greed. I didn't give a shit when Melanie was fucking that Sergeant Major, and I certainly didn't give a shit when I slit her wrists. The only thing I cared about was the mess I was gonna have to clean up after I put that bitch down. Using the bathtub was a nice touch, don't cha think?"

"Great. Let Lily go and we can take a walk down memory lane, hold hands, and reminisce about old times," Jasper smartassed. "What do you want, Roman?"

"That's the best question yet. And imagine, it came from the dumbest one on the team. But it's not so much about what I want as it's about what you all are willing to do to save Little Miss Sunshine. You see, I've been saving her for the perfect moment. Do any of you know how hard it's been keeping her a secret? Knowing I could take her out anytime I wanted? The sweet victory knowing I had Lenox's woman."

"What the fuck do you want, Roman?" I growled, trying to ignore Roman's taunts.

"There, there, lover boy. It is simple really. Lily will be taking a little vacation of sorts while I tend to a business deal. When the deal is complete, she'll be free to go. It's that simple."

A business deal.

Sick fuck acted like he was trading stocks, not selling weapons of mass destruction.

"Why now? You've been conducting *business* for years without taking hostages," Clark asked.

"Hostage? Why do you have to be so crass, Clark? Lily is not a hostage. She is my guest and guarantee you fuckers will turn a blind eye. This isn't just any deal. And the men I am delivering to need the extra reassurance that no one will disrupt our meeting. When the meeting is over, she'll be on the next plane back to the states."

That was total bullshit. The moment his deal was complete he'd kill Lily and be on the run again.

"Do you really think the 707 gives a shit if Lily lives or dies? She is expendable as far as they are concerned. Taking you out is all they care about," Clark helpfully explained.

"That doesn't sound like my problem. I'm sure Lenox would disagree about his girl being disposable. I'm sure you all think you're pretty smart, you can come up with something. Either way, I don't really care. If you want Lily to live, you'll figure it out. Besides, you don't really have an option. Any of you fuck this up for me, I will find another bargaining chip. You all have someone in your past you want to protect. I found Lenox's, you think I can't find yours?" Roman addressed Clark and Jasper.

I'd had enough.

Roman continued to taunt Clark and Jasper, not that they gave two fucks what he threatened. We all knew Roman was not leaving here alive. Instead I focused on Lily's wide scared eyes. I had to make a decision and I prayed I wasn't signing Lily's death warrant. There was only one way out of this situation. My eyes bore into hers and I nodded my head, hoping she could read my silent communication.

Turning my attention back to Roman, my field of vision tunneled to the immediate. My breathing steadied, my heart rate slowed. My weapon was merely an extension of my hand, and in one continuous motion, my finger slid down the cool metal of the trigger guard and I waited for Lily's body to go limp. Her knees gave way and she crumbled to the ground. Before Roman could register what had happened, I fired.

In that moment there were two choices, shoot to kill or shoot to harm. Normally I would've taken the one shot, one kill approach, but I wanted to play with him before I ended his life.

The vibration of the shot still coursed through my hands as I holstered my weapon and rushed to Lily, kicking Roman's weapon in the direction of Clark. I helped Lily get to her feet and passed her trembling body to Jasper. I pulled my knife from my vest as I knelt down next to Roman. With a flick of my thumb, the blade came free from the bolster. I tried to steady my hand from the rush of adrenaline, or maybe it was excitement, as I pressed my blade against his throat.

"A bullet would be too easy you, motherfucker," I whispered as I sank the tip of the knife into the left side of his throat.

Roman tried to scream, but the sound that came out was garbled as blood oozed from his neck.

"You got something to say? Not so talkative now that you have my bullet in your shoulder and my blade in your throat."

"As much as I would love to watch you torture this fucktard, we have to leave," Jasper said.

Jasper was right.

I wanted to draw this out, spending hours craving his insides out and watching him suffer for the fear he put in Lily, but we didn't have time.

"See you in hell, fucker."

I slowly sank the blade further into the side of his throat, the handle of my knife warming as Roman's blood coated my hand. With a twist of my wrist, I watched as the life drained from his face and his eyes dimmed.

One less scumbag to roam the earth.

I didn't spare Roman's dead body a second look, he wasn't worth the air he sucked from the room. I would feel no remorse for taking his life, I never did when I put a dog down. He was simply another hash mark on my soul. My only concern now was getting Lily off this island.

I swept Lily up into my arms and ran for the door, Levi following closely behind covering us. I heard Jasper and Clark behind us, one of them calling the boat to pick us up. As soon as my foot hit the wood of the dock, the boat came to a stop at the end. One of the men jumped out to steady the boat as we each jumped aboard. With an easy push off the dock, the boat sped away.

Even with miles now between us and Roman's

cay, Lily remained in my arms trembling. The relief I felt was eye-opening. I had almost lost her. And not in a way where I'd push her away so she could go on without me. The dead kind. Roman could've very easily killed her. What the hell had I done? She belonged to me. I'd give up all of this, anything, if I could have her.

She hadn't made a sound, she hadn't shed a tear, she was damn near catatonic as I wiped the blood spatter off her face.

"Lily, you need to drink some water," Clark said offering her a bottle.

Wordlessly she took the bottle and drank.

Jasper, Levi, and Clark all had identical pissed off looks. Each of them had berated me over the last few weeks, telling me that I was a dick for leaving Lily. They were right. I was a cold-hearted dick, but I thought I would rather be a dick than the selfish bastard who left Lily a widow, or worse, got her killed. I thought I loved her enough to give her up.

I was wrong.

19

How had my life come to this? The last month had been a whirlwind of emotions. First, I found out that Shane was alive, him coming out of the shadows just in time to save me from two would-be assailants. Then I spent the most glorious week with Shane, all the while my mental state fluctuated from overwhelming joy to bone-crushing fear. And finally, immense pain when he left again. An agony that was incomparable, one that I have barely survived the last three weeks. The coup de gras was being kidnapped by a crazy man and used as a pawn in some twisted game of cat and mouse. I was the mouse in that equation, and Roman would've had no issue killing me if Shane hadn't killed him first. I should've felt bad he was dead, but I didn't. Somewhere in my subconscious I wondered if that made me a bad person. At the end of the day, I really didn't care.

I sat and wondered what it would've been like if Shane had never come back into my life. If I could make a wish and go back in time, would I? Rewind time when I thought he was dead and I was grieving my best friend. When I'd never met Lenox. As hard as I tried to summon up regret and anger, I couldn't. If he'd never come back, I wouldn't have the baby I'm growing. Now, when he leaves I will always have a part of him with me. He'll never know, but I will.

"Lily, do you want a beer?" Jasper asked when he walked out onto the balcony of the condo we were currently staying in.

"No thank you," I answered.

"That's two nights in a row. You want a whiskey instead?" he tried.

"I'm too tired for alcohol, Jasper. I'll fall right to sleep," I lied.

I looked back at the ocean hoping he would stop questioning why I wasn't drinking. When we were staying in Big Bear I never turned down the offer of a drink.

"You know if you need to talk I'm here," he offered.

Talking was the last thing I needed. I needed a

lobotomy or eye bleach. I don't think I would ever stop dreaming about the things I have seen in the last few days. Hell, the last month. All this started with two dead guys at the cemetery and the body count only went up from there.

Clark had already drilled me about my time spent with Calvin, or Roman, whatever they wanted to call him. I explained about Peter and James. The explosion that came after they found out James was a traitor and Peter died trying to keep me safe was loud and scary. I skipped the part about Roman's threats. I didn't think they were important. He was dead after all and couldn't carry out anything he promised.

Levi pushed for answers about my time spent on the island before they arrived. By the grace of God, it was uneventful and Roman left me alone. He had me trapped, surrounded by water. It wasn't like I could escape and swim a hundred miles to Cuba. And luckily for him I was a little rusty on my raft building skills. Actually, I barely saw Roman once we got there. The bruise on my cheek was from one of his guards. He had tried to touch me and I spit in his face, earning me a back hand. Roman killed him, too. Yet another body I'd have to sort through later. I was afraid if I tried to process everything that had happened now, I would have a come apart, only further delaying my departure. And I needed to get away from Shane and his team as soon as possible.

"I'm fine, really. I'm happy that Roman is gone and I can go back to my normal life."

Lies, lies, and more lies. That is what my life had come to - lies. I lied to the guys, I lied to Shane, and I was most definitely lying to myself. Truth was I would never be alright again.

Jasper looked over his shoulder. I caught the lift of his chin before he got up and Shane took his place in the chair next to mine.

"Lily, we need to talk," Shane said.

Oh goody, more talking. I could barely contain my laughter. That was exactly what we didn't need.

"I don't think there is anything left to say, Lenox. You were crystal clear at the cabin."

"I've asked you to stop calling me that. You call me Shane."

"No. I did until you reminded me that Shane is dead. I've accepted that. I had twelve years to mourn his death, and now it's time I move on."

I prayed I could pull off the cool, blasé attitude. The faster this was over, the quicker I could go to my room and cry in peace. Hormones, that was all this was, I tried to remind myself.

"I'm sorry. I need to tell you the truth," he started.

"Don't be." I pushed off the chair and stood almost knocking it over. "You already told me the truth. It's not your fault it wasn't the answer I wanted."

"You need to listen to me. I lied..."

Ignoring his last statement, I went on. "After I had time to think about what you had said, you were right. I only thought I loved you, all those memories of us as kids clouded my feelings. There is nothing between us. There never was. I had a silly high school crush on you, that's all it was. I should be the one to apologize to you for making an ass out of myself. My flight leaves in the morning. I'll be out of your hair for good." I closed my eyes and took a long cleansing breath before walking to the sliding glass door. "Thank you for everything you've done for me. Goodbye, Lenox."

"Lily, please," he yelled after me.

I didn't stop or look back as I walked through the small condo to the front door. I needed some fresh air. I was no longer under house arrest now that Roman was dead. Me staying in Nassau was only because I was waiting for my passport to arrive. Now that I had it, my flight was booked and I was ready to leave. I was sure it was Clark's idea to stay here with me. Levi and Jasper were both walking on eggshells, and both looked totally uncomfortable to be in the same room as me. They'd all be off the hook soon.

I wasn't going back to California. I didn't want to raise my child in the city. Rebecca was about to be the proud owner of McGrath Carter. I sent my attorney an email and asked him to have the paperwork drawn up. She would do right by the people the centers served. She had a heart for service. I was happy to give them to her.

I wasn't sure where I would end up - I needed time to figure that out. The plan was to start in Texas and go from there. I had enough money to live comfortably, but I would eventually need to get a job. I'd wait until later to figure that out - one step at a time.

"You need to tell him."

I nearly fell into the sand when I heard the voice behind me.

"No, I don't. And you won't either," I replied.

"Why? Give me one good reason not to tell Lenox that you're carrying his kid?" Jasper asked.

Smart, observant bastard.

"Because he'll stay," I answered honestly.

"Isn't that what you want? Isn't that his choice?"

I turned to look at Jasper. His normal playful attitude was gone. He looked so serious with his eyebrows scrunched up and a thoughtful expression.

"No. I want him to love me as much as I love him. I want him to stay with me because he cannot imagine his life without me in it. I don't want to be an obligation. I love him too much to have him grow to resent me. And if he gives up his team, he will. He'll resent me and the baby, and I already love this child too much to watch that happen."

As painful as the truth was, that was it. I was willing to carry the burden of guilt so Shane would be happy. "He said it himself, he doesn't think he can be a good husband and operator. We both know what his first love is."

"He loves you," Jasper said.

"I know he does. And I have loved him since I was sixteen years old. I never, not for one day, stopped loving him. When I leave here tomorrow, I will continue to love him for all the days I have left. That's why you need to keep my secret. Let him go on and be happy."

I almost choked on my words. I was trying to be strong and not a selfish bitch trapping Shane into a life he clearly didn't want. But it was taking all my strength not to run to him and beg him to stay with me and the baby.

"He'll find out, and when he does, he'll be pissed. Rightfully so."

"I'm not going back to LA. He'll never see us again. Please, Jasper, try and understand. I begged him not to leave me. His response was to tell me about all the women he's fucked over the years, how what we shared was meaningless, and he only wanted to get me out of his system." Jasper winced as I spoke. "He doesn't want me. I am begging you not to tell. Let me and the baby be happy."

"I can't promise I will keep your secret forever. But, I will keep it for now. You both need time. I know he loves you, he is being stubborn. The thing you have to understand is he truly thinks he is letting you go to protect you. He is afraid that he will put you in danger."

"Thank you. And I am sorry I didn't get to say thank you or goodbye when you left Big Bear. I missed you all when you were gone. I hope you can fix or make peace with whatever is making you so sad. You're a really great guy. I'd hate to see you live the rest of your life lonely and unhappy."

Jasper's body went stiff and he stood to his full height, a hard look crossed his face.

"You should mind your own business, Lily."

"You're right, I should. But what kind of friend would I be if I didn't acknowledge your pain? I lived in constant sadness for twelve years, I allowed my life to pass me by. No more. You should think about doing the same - let go of the past and live your life." I turned back toward the water. "We only have one."

Jasper would either keep my secret or he wouldn't. I couldn't worry about that right now. I had a plane to catch and a life to begin.

I guess what they say is true, it's never too late to start.

20

"What the fuck were you thinking?" Clark screamed at me when I jumped into the van after I tossed a tied-up Miguel Nunez in.

"I was thinking I was tired of sitting outside of a goddamn whorehouse while this prick got his rocks off. What the hell is it with scumbags liking to bang prostitutes? He's alive, mission accomplished. One drug dealer delivered," I shouted back. I was sick and tired of sitting outside of whorehouses.

I was getting really fed up having to explain my every move to Clark. In the five months since we left Lily at the airport in Nassau, we've been on four back-to-back missions. I had yet to be stateside. I was tired and wanted to see the inside of my own bedroom sometime in the near future.

"You're dangerous, Lenox. You need to pull your head out of your ass before you get yourself dead," he continued to chastise me.

Death would be easier than the constant ache I felt. If I was being honest, death was actually preferable to this pain. Not that I would tell that to the fucking safety police.

"What can I say? I like living on the edge."

"Jesus Christ..."

"Enough," Jasper yelled.

The rest of the trip back to the compound was done in silence. As soon as we pulled through the barbed wire gates and came to a stop, I threw the back doors open of the van and jumped out. I didn't want to be around anybody. Fuck, I didn't even want to be around myself.

I pulled the mosquito netting back from my bunk and threw myself on the rickety metal bed. I was fucking exhausted and needed to sleep.

"We need to talk," Jasper slammed the door behind him.

"Man, I'm not in the mood," I replied.

Now was not the time for another ass chewing. I wanted to lie in my bed and wallow in my self-pity. I fucked up bad. I hurt Lily, and now she wouldn't even talk to me. And yes, I had tried to call her. The number was disconnected and I had no resources to find her while I was stuck in this godforsaken third world country.

"Too bad. You wanna kill yourself, not my business. You pull stupid shit while we're on a mission and put the team in jeopardy again, we'll have a big fuckin' problem," Jasper said. "It's been five months. We all know that your head is screwed up. No one wants to bring Lily up..."

"Enough, Jasper. Don't even say her name to me," I growled.

"Fix your head, brother, or Lily will be a non-issue because you'll be dead. Then what? She'll spend the next twelve years at another cemetery? Only this time there'll be no coming back. I don't need to tell you how badly you screwed up because you're beatin' yourself up enough. Just fix your shit and get your girl."

He didn't wait for a response before he left, leaving me in silence. He was mostly right, but wrong about Lily visiting the cemetery. After what I said to her she wouldn't bother going to visit. She was done with me.

The musty smell of humidity and stale air hit me as soon as I walked through my front door. It had been damn near six months since I'd been home. I really needed to hire someone from base to come over and open my house up while I was gone. I walked around my sad living room opening all the windows.

I tried to imagine Lily here in this house. She'd hate it. It was plain and boring, absolutely no personal effects anywhere in the room. After I faked my death, I stopped living. Shane was dead not only on paper but in my mind as well. There was no me without Lily. It was easy to slip into my role as Lenox. Lenox didn't know Lily; he didn't know what it felt like to laugh with her, the feel of her cuddled up on the couch watching movies, and he didn't know what it felt like to love her. Carter Lenox was literally a soulless bastard.

I tossed my bag in the laundry room and opened the fridge, nothing.

"Fuck," I roared to the empty room.

I hated my life. Loved my job, but hated the loneliness that came with it. If Lily were here, the house would be warm and inviting. There would be food in the fridge when I came home from a long work trip. She would have soft sheets on our bed and fresh towels in the bathroom. I could picture her taking a warm bath in the big tub in the master bedroom with the flowery candles she loves burning while she soaked in bubbles.

I heard a knock at the front door and my heart skipped a beat until I remembered Lily didn't know where I lived. She wouldn't seek me out and surprise me the day I came home. I had no one. The pounding on the front door continued and I debated not answering. It was probably the neighbor with a box of my mail.

"Open up, I know your sorry ass is in there," Jasper yelled.

Jesus! Can't a man get two minutes of peace and quiet? We'd spent the last five months trekking through the underbelly of the world. Wasn't he sick of seeing my face already? I know I was.

"It's open," I called back not bothering to leave the kitchen.

Jasper walked through the door with two pizzas, followed by Clark with a case of beer, and Levi picked up the rear with a bottle of Jack Daniels.

I was about to tell them to get out when the smell of the pizza wafted through the room making me reconsider my position on company. This would save me a much-needed trip to the store tonight.

The guys beelined it for the kitchen table, and I grabbed some paper plates and paper towels. How sad was my life that at thirty-two years old I didn't have proper tableware?

"Miss me already?" I joked as I threw the paper plates on the table.

Levi, not bothering to wait, already had a beer open and a slice in his mouth.

"Call this rendition and reprogramming," Clark said opening the bottle of Jack Daniels and sliding it across the table to me.

"Rendition, huh? Why am I being interrogated?"

"What are your intentions with Lily?" Jasper smirked and took a bite of his pizza like he didn't just toss gasoline on a fire.

"Not your business," I replied, picking up the bottle of Jack. Three gulps later I still couldn't feel the burn of the liquor. I was back to being numb. In the past twelve years, I had been able to feel for exactly eight days.

"That's where you are wrong, friend. It is my business," he shot back.

"How do you figure that?" I asked.

"You made it our business when you brought Lily to us in California. It further became our business when you told us that we were to treat Lily with respect. Even more so when you threatened to kill me if I ever called her a piece of ass again because she was your world," Clark interjected.

"And it became my business when you gutted that woman like she was no better than a third world hooker. You fucked her, told her you loved her, then you shattered her soul," Jasper informed me.

"Watch your mouth, *friend*, you'll be smart never to compare Lily to a two-bit whore again," I snarled. "You all are dangerously close to crossing a line."

"Man, we passed that line about five hundred meters ago. We are so far over the line and it's so blurry there is no line. So what are you going to do about Lily?" Jasper pushed.

We sat in silence for a long while. The guys sat at my table eating pizza and drinking beer like it was a regular poker night, and not like my life was in ruins. I was debating whether or not to be honest with them or keep this bottled up. These men were my brothers. We faced death together, but when it came to feelings, those were never talked about. As much as I hated to admit it, I needed help.

"I fucked up. Not only did I burn that bridge, I blew it up. Completely and totally FUBAR'd," I admitted.

"Bullshit, nothing is beyond repair. You wanna fix it?" Jasper asked.

"Yes," I answered honestly. "I want her here with me. My head is so screwed up I can't think straight. It's killing me knowing I hurt her, and now I've lost her. I never should've let her go. She begged me not to do it, but I didn't listen. I thought I was doing it for her own good. I was wrong."

It had to have been the Jack that caused the moisture in the corner of my eyes. The liquor was making my lips loose and my eyes watery.

"I had a daughter," Jasper started.

Levi stopped his beer half way to his mouth and stared at Jasper like he had grown three heads.

"How did we not know that?" I was in shock. Jasper had never once mentioned her.

"She would've been three."

"Three?" Clark, Levi, and I asked in unison.

"Remember when I went home on leave when my granddad passed?" He waited for us all to acknowledge we remembered. "I saw my ex-girlfriend, Liz. Two months after I'm back here she calls me and tells me she's pregnant. I fucked up and questioned if the baby was mine. After a whole lot of crying and arguing, she tells me to fuck off and hangs up. I never called back."

Jasper stopped and hung his head in shame. When he lifted his head again, he didn't try and hide his pain. "By the time I got my head out of my ass it was too late. You wanna know why I didn't call back? I thought they would be better off without me. My job would get in the way of me being a good dad or husband. I loved her and that baby, but I was too much of a coward to admit it."

I knew Jasper had demons he was fighting. Thinking back, it was right after his grandfather died that he changed. I thought the change was because his grandfather raised him and they were close.

"How did she die?" Levi whispered.

"Alesha, my daughter, was stillborn. Liz died giving birth to her."

"Man, I am so sorry. You should've told us, we would've helped you through it," I told him.

"Don't wait like I did. Make it right with Lily now," he urged.

The pizza lay abandoned in the middle of the table and the bottle of whiskey was passed around. Each of us lost in thought. I caught Jasper giving me sidelong glances, and by the time the bottle of whiskey was almost empty, guilt looked to be weighing heavily on him.

"What aren't you telling me?" I asked.

Jasper averted his gaze suddenly, finding the table extremely interesting. Something was very wrong. "Is Lily okay?"

"No," he answered.

"No?" I shot up from my seat uncaring I had knocked the chair over. "Talk, Jasper."

"Before I tell you, you need to take a seat and relax."

"Fuck that noise. Tell me," I demanded.

"Lily's pregnant."

I closed my eyes, and fought to stay upright. I was too late, she'd moved on and she was having a baby.

"The baby is yours," Jasper continued.

"What?" I gasped when I caught my breath. "How do you know?"

"I knew when we were in Nassau."

Without thinking, I charged Jasper. "Motherfucker."

Clark jumped from his seat and wrapped his arms around my middle, preventing me from getting to the lying rat bastard.

"Calm the fuck down," Clark demanded.

"You all knew?" I yelled.

"I agreed to keep her secret for your own good," Jasper yelled back.

Clark let me go and shoved me away from him. "Settle down and listen to him. He was right in keeping this from you."

I struggled to keep my temper in check. I was going to kill the asshole for keeping my child a secret, but I needed to know what he knew first.

"Lily is pregnant with my child, and you think he was right for not telling me? My child could've grown up without a father." I had been so reckless in the last few months I could've died and left Lily to raise our child alone.

"You think we would've let your dumb ass get dead?" Levi asked.

I shot Levi a glare that couldn't have been misinterpreted as anything other than the "fuck you" it was meant to be.

"Lily needed time to heal, and she didn't need any added stress being newly pregnant," Jasper explained. "I told her I wouldn't keep her secret forever because you needed to know. But you both needed to get your heads on straight before one of you fucked up and did something you couldn't take back. The last thing you needed was to know about the baby. You would've pushed her."

"Goddamn right I would've pushed. She's having my baby."

"She didn't want you to resent her, and she was afraid that you would only be staying with her because of the baby."

"Is she crazy? I fucking love her."

I needed a plan. Lily being pregnant didn't change a damn thing for me. What it did do was move the timeline along. I was planning a slow attack, move so slow she didn't realize what I was doing until it was too late and she loved me again. Now it was going to be a full court press, an out and out war of hearts.

"Crazy? You told her you didn't love her. We heard exactly what you said to her," Levi put his two cents in.

"You're right, I did. We all know I fucked up. What do I do now?" I asked the room at large and paced back and forth.

I was still going to kick Jasper's ass just as soon as I had my family tucked safely in my home. But right now, I had more important things to worry about.

"We go to her," Clark answered.

"We?"

"Man, you're gonna need all the backup you can use. When you show up on her doorstep, she is going to toss your sorry ass out the door. Luckily for you, she seems to like me. I'll put in a good word for you." Clark smirked.

I didn't have time to dissect the bullshit he said, but his plan did have merit. No doubt I would need help.

"Maybe you should hang back." I pointed to Jasper. "She's gonna be pissed you told her secret and that woman holds a mean grudge. You might fuck up my chances. And Jasper, after I sort out Lily, I'm gonna beat your sorry ass for not telling me." Jasper laughed like I was joking. I wasn't, she could stay mad forever if she wanted to.

"Looking forward to it, asshole," Jasper shot back still laughing.

"Now, I have to find her." I grabbed my laptop off the coffee table and turned it on. I had planned to start my search for her in the morning, but now seemed like a good time.

"I already found her," Levi informed me.

"You didn't think you could've started the night off with that tidbit." I slammed my laptop lid shut.

What the hell was wrong with my team? All these goddamn secrets.

"Nope. A little extra suffering is good for the soul." He chuckled and pulled a folded piece of paper out of his pocket and handed it to me.

I opened the folded paper and scanned the information. There was an address in South Carolina and a phone number. "Lillian and Carter Lenox? I don't understand."

"Congratulations, it's a boy. I hacked her obstetrician's records and read through the notes. It looks like she already named him Carter."

"I have a son," I sighed.

I'm coming for you Lily. You and my boy.

21

"Hi, Lily. How are you making out?" Miss Milly the shopkeeper asked.

Now in my third trimester, I finally settled on a place to call home: Myrtle Beach, South Carolina. I found a cute bungalow on the beach that offered a long-term rental. I loved it. It even had a wooden boardwalk down to the surf, and tall sand grass surrounded the house. It looked to be straight out of a movie.

I had traveled across the US the last five months. I started in Texas and went North. I considered staying in Montana, it was stunning there, but I quickly realized I am a beach girl at heart. I never wanted to step foot in California again, so I went East and landed in South Carolina. Good weather, good food, and great people. I didn't go East to be closer to Shane, at least that's what I repeated to myself every morning I woke up and thought about him and how easy it would be to drive a few hours South and be in Georgia.

We were done. He had made it clear that he didn't want me in his life. My head was starting to get on board with the idea of never seeing him again, but my heart refused to believe it. It hurt every day.

"Lily?" Milly's voice pulled me from my wayward thoughts.

"Sorry. I'm a little scatterbrained today. I'm all settled into the house, but still trying to get the lay of the land," I admitted.

"I remember what it's like being pregnant. They say the baby takes all of the mother's brain power." Milly giggled. "The paint supplies you ordered will be here tomorrow. Would you like me to deliver them?"

I was going to try my hand at painting. I had never done it before, but I needed something to occupy my time. Five hours of Bob Ross YouTube instruction later, I felt confident I could be a master painter in no time. I could've ordered my supplies online or driven to a big box store and bought what I needed for cheaper, but I wanted to support the local shops if I could. Miss Milly was a sweet older woman. If I had to guess, I'd say she was almost seventy, especially since she talked about her adult grandchildren. She had a large family and was very proud when she spoke about them. I felt a pang of jealousy and a huge heap of guilt. I never had a close, loving family and my son would never have a large, tight-knit family either.

"Are you okay? Did I say something to upset you?" Milly asked.

"Oh no, Miss Milly. I'm sorry, I really am lost in thought today," I replied.

"If you don't mind me saying, you look like you need a friend." Milly came out from behind the counter. She was a small woman, but the fierce look on her face told me she was not someone who took no for an answer.

"I really am okay. I think I overdid it a little yesterday. I unpacked the rest of my boxes last night. But it's nothing a good night's sleep won't cure. I only walked down here to pick up some more of your delicious peaches. I can't seem to get enough of them." I gave her what I hoped was a reassuring smile.

"I had a new delivery this morning, fresh from a local grower in Georgia. There's nothing like a sweet

Georgia peach." My body stiffened and tears formed in my eyes at the mention of Georgia.

Maybe staying here was not going to be such a good idea. I can't even eat my favorite peaches without being reminded of Shane. Not that getting away from the peaches would help me forget about him. In a moment of utter weakness, I legally changed my name to Lenox. Dumb, dumb, dumb. I was so stupid. I thought about changing it to something else, but Shane's last name was the only thing I could give my son from his father. I couldn't bring myself to deny either of them that connection, even if I was the only one who knew.

"Young lady, you are looking pale. I am sending my grandson over this evening with a lasagna and peach cobbler. You need some home cooking and rest. I'll send Adam around about six this evening."

"Oh no, Miss Milly, that is very kind of you to offer, but I can't put you out like that."

"Nonsense, child, I wouldn't have offered if I wasn't happy to do it. Besides, I miss cooking for a family. It will be my pleasure. And just so you know, it's rude to turn down an old woman's offer of food around here."

"Well alright, I wouldn't want to be rude," I

laughed. "But, please don't inconvenience your grandson. I'll come by and pick it up."

"Now that would defeat the purpose. You're supposed to be relaxing." She leveled me with her best motherly glare.

"Yes, ma'am. Thank you again, it has been a long time since I've had a real home cooked meal."

"Well, mine are made with love. We call it soul food in my home, because after your tummy is good and full from all that love I sprinkle in there, you can't help but be happy," she explained with a wink.

"I am quite certain I've never had a meal sprinkled with love. The cooks that my father hired were there for the money, not the love."

"That is downright sad. It's settled, I'll sprinkle in some extra love for you. Now go on and get your peaches and get home. You look tired."

"Thank you."

I'm sure I did look tired, but I didn't need confirmation on just how haggard I looked. I had hoped I was able to hide the dark circles under my eyes with concealer, but apparently not. The nightmares I'd been having were coming far and few between now. The first couple of months after I got back to the US I dreamt of dead bodies every night. Surprisingly, Roman's death was not one I had nightmares about even though he was killed while using me as a human shield.

I didn't know if it was because I felt relief he was dead and my baby was safe, or if it was because I saw the love and determination in Shane's eyes when he pulled the trigger. He killed Roman to protect me, to save my life. All the others were senseless and brutal. I thought about Peter a lot and how kind he was to me. In the short time I spent with him, he became a friend of sorts. While he didn't share any of his life with me, he listened while I cried about Shane. I felt the loss of him deeply.

The walk back to my bungalow was quick. Milly's shop was only a few blocks down, and it was a perfect afternoon for a stroll. The small streets were beautiful, and the locals and tourists alike were friendly and always waved as you passed. Something that was unheard of in busy Los Angeles. You could barely go to a bank these days without bulletproof glass between you and the teller. Somehow, I couldn't imagine that glass barrier here.

It was too nice of a day to spend indoors. I grabbed my beach chair and Kindle and headed for the beach. There was nothing better than getting lost in the pages of a good book. I could forget my pathetic life and be transported to the *Stone Society's* post-apocalyptic world where sexy five-hundred-year-old gargoyle shapeshifters rule the land and save the girl. I desperately wished someone like *Rafael* or *Gregor* would sweep in and save me from my sad, lonely existence. I giggled to myself thinking about what it would be like to have a sexy shapeshifter sweep me off my feet and profess his undying love and loyalty. I'm sure those men know their way around the bedroom, too. My overactive imagination could easily conjure up the sexy Rafael taking me... nope, not going there. Damn pregnancy hormones either had me in tears or dreaming about sex.

"Lily?" I heard a man's voice calling out my name, pulling me from the most delicious dream. Shane and Gregor were rescuing me from a sinister vampire that wanted to turn me to the dark side. Neither of the men had shirts on as they fought the vampire, muscles flexed and sweat ran over the ridges of their cut abs. Both men fighting over who was going to claim me as their mate.

"I'm sorry, are you Lily?" the man asked again. I cracked my eyes open and tried to focus on his face.

"Yes, I'm Lily," I answered.

"I'm Adam. My grandmother Milly sent me over with dinner. Sorry I'm a little early, she didn't want it to get cold."

"Dinner? What time is it?" I asked, trying to push myself off my chair which was becoming harder and harder to do with a beach ball for a belly.

"Five-thirty. Here let me help you up," Adam said.

"Thank you." I grabbed his outstretched hand and pulled myself up. "I can't believe I fell asleep out here."

I hoped I hadn't been snoring or drooling, how embarrassing. I tried to smooth my sundress, more to keep my hands busy than anything else. Now that I was standing, I could see how handsome Miss Milly's grandson was. Holy wow, he was hot.

"Good thing I came when I did. Another little while and the mosquitoes would've made a meal outta you." Adam winked.

Holy shit, was he flirting with me? No, of course, he wasn't. I was very obviously knocked up, and I'm sure I looked a mess.

"I'm sorry you had to drive all this way to bring me food. I offered to pick it up. I hope it wasn't too much of an imposition."

"None at all. I actually only live two houses down." Adam pointed to a sea green cottage one house over than the one I was renting. "I left the food on the porch. Do you want me to carry your chair back to the house or are you staying out here?"

"I think I've had enough sun for one day. But, I can carry my chair," I said as I folded it up and picked my Kindle up out of the sand.

"I'll take the chair, it's the gentlemanly thing to do." Adam's face broke into a wide smile.

"And are you a gentleman?" I smiled back.

"Not according to my boyfriend, Anthony. But he likes the bad boys, so it works."

Sigh. So much for some harmless flirting to get my mind off of my heartbreak. He had a boyfriend.

"Being a gentleman is overrated. I'm with Anthony - there's nothing hotter than a bad boy who means business." I laughed at my stupid reply. I really needed to make friends and get out more. I had been in isolation so long I had forgotten how to carry on a conversation without making an ass out of myself.

Adam took the folded chair and started for the house. "How do you like the area so far?"

How did he know I am new to the area? Was I still being followed, did Roman still have people watching me?

Adam must've noticed my confusion. "Gran said

you just moved here. There is nothing like small town old biddies who gossip."

Milly. I forgot, Milly knew I just moved here.

"It's beautiful here. So much different than California."

When we got to the porch, Adam held the screen door open for me to walk through. "Why, how gentlemanly of you."

"Please don't tell Anthony. I don't want him catching on."

"Your secret is safe with me. Wow. That is a big lasagna." I commented on the huge casserole dish.

"That's Gran. Go big or go home."

"Oh, are you all originally from Texas?" I asked. I didn't think I detected a Texas twang, but Milly's South Carolina drawl was so thick it was hard to tell.

"Hell no. Born and raised here in South Carolina. Gran just likes to feed the people she loves. I guess it's a southern thing. I spend many extra hours in the gym after Sunday dinner."

"Well, I can tell you that the extra gym time is workin' for ya." My hands shot to my mouth, but it was too late. "I can't believe I said that out loud. I'm so sorry."

I was going to die of humiliation. If the universe

was ever going to open up and swallow me whole, now would be the perfect time.

"Yep, you said that out loud alright. I'm mighty pleased you think so, ma'am." Adam tucked his chin and nodded as if he was tipping an invisible hat or something.

"Now you're laying it on thick, aren't you? Stupid pregnancy brain. Sorry, I'm normally very shy. Guess you lose your social filter when you're always alone."

"Why is a beautiful woman like you alone?" he asked.

"Long boring story," I sighed.

"I got time for a long boring story if you feel like sharing. Anthony is bartending tonight until nine. I am a free agent for another three hours."

"You may need three years," I mumbled under my breath.

"Now you have to tell me. I'm officially inviting myself in for story time and some of Gran's famous lasagna." Adam picked up the dishes and motioned for me to open the front door.

"How do I know you're not crazy?" I asked only half joking.

"Do you think that sweet old woman would send a crazy person to your house?" he laughed.

"Well, you are her grandson. She might overlook your crazy if she loves you." I was shocked at how easy it was to talk to Adam. And I really could use some company. It was lonely sitting by myself night after night.

"Have you met my grandmother? That woman tells it like she sees it. Grandson or not, she'd call me on my crazy."

I opened the door and allowed Adam to walk past me, turning to the left to go to the kitchen. Something struck me as odd.

"Have you been in here before?" I asked.

"Yep. I did the remodel before I flipped it and sold it," he told me. "That's what Anthony and I do. We have a bunch of properties up and down the East coast. We buy mostly foreclosures, or bail home-owners out of their mortgages before they go into default. We remodel, update when necessary, and flip them. We've kept a few as rental properties, and we have two that we use as personal residences. And then there's Gran's house, too. We bought a cute one-bedroom cottage and built an extension for the new kitchen and dining room. Those are the only two rooms she cares about. Someplace to cook family dinners and somewhere to serve them. We were able to give her a small green space out back for her to garden, but nothing so big she can't take care of it herself."

"That was so kind of you to do that for your gran." I was stunned. I knew a few friends who were close to their families, but in the world, I grew up in, it was rare to see that kind of devotion for a grandparent.

The mere fact that I was even thinking that scared me. Maybe I wasn't fit to be a good mom. I didn't even have one growing up. I had nannies that were paid to keep an eye on me, not love or nurture me. I was going to screw this up. I had no business doing this in general, but most especially alone.

"Hey? Where'd you go?" Adam asked.

"I was thinking how lucky you were to have such a great family. I didn't have that. I was surrounded by cooks, and maids, and nannies. No one loved me or taught me how to be a good mom. And now I'm having this baby, and I'm afraid I should start saving for my son's therapy now. God knows I'm gonna screw this all up. I'm so dumb to think I could do this by myself."

Adam cut into the lasagna and plated it up before setting a heaping piece of cheesy goodness in front of me. He still hadn't said a word. I bet he wished he was the one to ask if I was the crazy one before he came in.

"I know we only met, and you don't know me. So, I'm gonna have to lay it out. I have zero filter and no social grace. I'm beyond pussy footing around. I blurt shit out. If that offends you, I apologize in advance." He stopped and waited for me to nod. "Great. So, why are you doing this alone? Where's the baby's daddy?"

Whoa. Talk about going for the gusto right off the bat. He was truthful, there definitely was no pussy footing around.

"That's the long story."

"Great. Start talking, and don't leave anything out, especially if he's hot. And you are absolutely gorgeous, so there is no doubt this baby daddy is fine."

"Do you want the novel or the cliff notes?" I asked.

"The novel, please. And don't forget the good parts, like the baby making." Adam wiggled his eyebrows and dug into his food.

"It all started when we were in high school..."

And that was how my friendship with Adam started. Lasagna, peach cobbler, and a whole lot of tears. He listened, and interjected, and gave his opinion. And boy, he was like his gran and held nothing back. He said he thought we were both wrong, and stubborn, and stupid.

That night I cried my eyes out. Not only was my heart broken, but I was drowning under the weight of my guilt.

Over the last week, I'd spent a lot of time with Adam and Anthony. They were both great guys and so funny. I had never laughed so hard in my life. I knew all about their families and childhoods. They told me more about their business and the charity work they did for Vets and the houses they remodeled for active duty military families as a way to give back to them. Both of them were giving, funny, and totally easy on the eyes. I hated they would be leaving soon to go South. They had a remodel and flip in Savannah. They asked me to tag along when they saw pictures of my condo in Los Angeles. Anthony thought I'd be great at staging their houses once they were ready to sell. But that was too close to Shane, and with the baby coming, I didn't want to travel. I was flattered they had asked.

We had just finished barbecuing hamburgers and

brought them in my kitchen. I was shaking up the ketchup bottle, laughing at Anthony's silly impression of Adam trying to paddle board when the top popped off the bottle and red sauce splattered all over Adam's shirt and face.

"Oh my God. I'm so sorry." I spat out half-laughing, half-horrified that I ruined his shirt.

"Oh, don't be sorry. Now he has to take his shirt off and eat his dinner bare chested. Well played, friend, well played." Anthony's comment only made me laugh harder, as if I'd done it on purpose.

Adam pulled the soiled shirt over his head and wiped his face with it.

"Here, let me rinse it out in the sink." I offered, taking the shirt from Adam. "Damn, I don't have any stain remover spray here."

"It's fine, don't worry about it. I've had that shirt a million years. Let's eat." Adam waved me off.

"You're such a liar. This is the new shirt you got at the mall. I'll get you a new one."

"Lillian, sweetheart. It's fine really. Anthony wasn't lying, he prefers the show." Adam winked at me and took a gigantic bite out of his burger, uncaring he was half-nude.

"Alright, it's gonna bother me, too. Give me the shirt, I'll run it home and spray it down and be back in a flash." Anthony took the shirt and headed for the door. "And don't eat all the watermelon, you little piggies. I want some of that."

"I knew that it was only a matter of time before his OCD kicked in," Adam laughed now as he eyed the platter of cut-up melon.

Anthony was smart to tell us not to eat it all. The last one Adam and I picked up from the farmer's market was gone before Anthony was done with his bartending shift.

"We should've told him to bring you back a shirt to put on," I said around a mouthful of burger. "This is so good." I groaned.

"Why? Does me standing here bare-chested do funny things to your insides," Adam smirked.

"Ha! My insides, not a chance. But Anthony's, yes. And our night will be cut short because he won't be able to stop imagining doing bad things with you. And frankly, it makes me want to gag when he drools over all those muscles you have going on." I waved my hand in the direction of his chest and laughed.

"Oh, Lily. You need a man." Adam flexed his muscles and laughed.

"She has a man." Came from the doorway of my kitchen. I spun around so quickly I stumbled back.

Adam reached out and pulled me to his chest right before I fell.

"She does? Funny, I've been over here every night, and I don't remember seeing a man," Adam said.

The growl that came next was both terrifying and sexy as hell.

"Did you just growl?" I asked.

"I'd appreciate it if you'd take your hands off my woman," Shane ordered.

I belatedly noticed three very pissed off men standing behind Shane. All standing legs shoulder width apart, arms crossed over their chest.

"Well, hellooo, who called in the badass brigade and forgot to invite me?" Anthony said as he joined us in the kitchen. "I was only gone a minute. What'd I miss?"

Now it was Adam's turn to growl at Anthony. My eyes rolled with impatience, and suddenly the room felt very small with all the male egos floating around.

"Can we put away some of the testosterone, please?" I asked the room.

"Who is that?" Anthony loudly whispered to Adam.

"Baby daddy," Adam whispered back just as loud. No doubt all the guys could hear them as well.

"Helloo. She said he was hot. But, honey, he is really hot. Do we like him?" Anthony continued to carry on the very annoying side conversation, leaving us all staring at them.

"Not sure. He hasn't grovelled yet. But you are getting some of those commando boots because they are sexy."

A smile played on Shane's lips obviously amused and no longer worried another man, with no shirt on I might add, had his arms wrapped around me.

"Can you not discuss your bedroom games in my kitchen, please?" I scolded.

Shane's eyes came to mine and my breath caught in my throat. He looked sad and tired. I should've been happy he was miserable after everything he had put me through, but I wasn't. I was even more heart-broken. His eyes left mine and traveled to where Adam's hands were on my very pregnant belly. I waited for him to look at me again, but he remained focused on the baby.

"What are you doing here, Shane?" I asked.

"Can we talk in private?" His eyes came up to meet mine.

"Not right now. I have dinner guests." I pulled

away from Adam and walked around the island. "And you." I pointed to Jasper. "You're a rat fink bastard."

"I told you I wouldn't keep your secret forever. I gave you both time to get over your shit and told him," Jasper explained.

No, he didn't just say that to me.

"Get over my shit? Is that what you call getting my heart ripped out of my chest?"

"I see I didn't wait long enough," he mumbled.

"You would be correct. It would take a thousand lifetimes to get over *my shit,*" I growled out.

"No, Lily. A thousand lifetimes still wouldn't be enough. You'll never get over it. Want to know why?" Jasper put his hand up to stop me from speaking. "Don't answer that. I'll tell you why. Because there is no getting over it. Shane has to fix it, he's the only one who can. Just like he'll never get over you or what you said to him. When two people are destined to be together and share the love that you two have, there is no getting over the other person. So I guess the question is are you ready to stop being stubborn and forgive him for being a stupid prick."

"Don't know about baby daddy yet, but we like him," Anthony whispered.

"This isn't happening. Please tell me that this is a nightmare."

Tears were already forming in my eyes. I was more confused than ever. I had been making progress accepting that Shane was lost to me forever. Adam and Anthony had almost convinced me I could be a good mother, and in time, the pain of losing him would fade to a dull ache. Now Shane and his band of brothers show up in my little hide-a-way and blow my world apart again.

"It's happening, Lily. And I'm not leaving without you," Shane spoke up.

"And if I don't want to go?" I asked.

"You do." Shane smiled.

Smug bastard.

"Really? I think I made myself clear in Nassau that I didn't want to go anywhere with you."

"You mean when you sat on the balcony and lied your ass off? That time? Or the time I was too much of a pussy to wade through your lies and call you out on it because I was scared you'd finally wised up and saw me for the man I really am? *Or* the time in Big Bear when I was an asshole and lied through my teeth, trying to get you to hate me. Because then I was just being a spineless coward too afraid I would fail you and you'd be better off with a man that didn't kill people for a living. Because that time you begged me to stay and told me you loved me. So which time are we talking about, Lillian?"

"The, umm, I guess..."

"That's what I thought. Or are we talking about when you came back to the US and changed your name to Lillian Lenox so you'd still have a part of me with you? Which I gotta tell you has a beautiful ring to it, but pisses me the fuck off. If you want my last name, you'll take it when you're my wife."

"You're an arrogant ass." I folded my hands over my chest. "And I already have it."

"Damn right I am. But I am *your* arrogant ass."

"We definitely like him," Adam said not trying to whisper this time.

"You're coming home with me," Shane said.

"I am home, jerk."

I really wished we didn't have an audience for this discussion. So far, I'd held my shit together, but it was becoming increasingly hard not to yell at him or start crying or beg him never to leave me again. Which would've been totally pathetic and embarrassing.

"Then, I'll move here."

"You can't live this far from the base." Now it was my turn to smirk. There problem solved.

"Non-issue. My re-enlistment is up in sixty days. I'm out," he replied, matching my smile.

"What? No! You can't quit your job. You love your team. I won't let you, Shane. All you ever wanted to do was be in the Army." Tears formed and spilled down my cheeks. "Nothing has changed. I won't let you stop being who you were meant to be. You'll hate me for it. That's why I left; you said that you couldn't be a husband and an operator at the same time. I won't let you choose. I don't want to be with you. You should go home and forget about me, you'll be better off. And take them with you." I pointed to Jasper, Levi, and Clark.

I couldn't be here anymore. Shane needed to leave, and I had to move. If I had any chance of getting over him, I couldn't live anywhere there were memories of him.

"Goodbye, Shane."

22

I watched Lily walk down the hall, leaving me standing in the kitchen with her friends. She looked absolutely stunning. I didn't think it was possible for her to get any more beautiful but she was. Seeing her pregnant did crazy things to me. I felt like I was ten feet tall and invincible knowing that my baby was growing in her belly.

Imagine my surprise when I walked in and found a guy in her kitchen telling her she needed a man. My temper exploded, and I saw red. When he caught Lily, the sight of her pressed up against his bare chest was enough for me to commit murder. The only thing that had saved his life was the fact he was very obviously gay and that the other man we saw leaving was his boyfriend.

"I'm Adam. This is Anthony," the bare-chested one said.

"I'm Lenox. This is Clark, Jasper, and Levi." I pointed to each one respectively.

I eyed Adam. He looked like he had something to say, but Anthony was shaking his head.

"Say it," I invited.

"I'm assuming you came here to get Lily back," Adam said.

Anthony looked like he'd choked down a lemon but crossed his arms over his chest and stood by his man. Their posture made it seem as if they were worried I was going to jump over the island and attack at any moment. Depending on his next words, I might've.

"You'd be right," I confirmed.

"Bout time. I was wondering when you'd show up. Hate to ask this, because you look like you can kick my ass. But, she told me about your fight, so I have to. You ready for her and the baby?"

I had to give it to the guy, he had brass balls questioning me about my intentions with Lily. I damn near took my own teammate's head off for asking the same question. I debated whether or not to tell the guy to mind his own business, but I didn't think that would be in my best interest at the moment. Clark was right, I needed all the back-up I could get. I decided on honesty instead.

"I screwed up by telling Lily she was better off without me. I royally fucked up telling her I didn't love her. I've loved that woman since we were in high school, but I was just too much of a pansy ass to claim her. That's done now. I'm willing to do anything to get her to forgive me and come home," I explained.

Adam seemed to mull over my words before he nodded his head. "You're gonna need some privacy and a pint of the banana ice cream; there's one in the freezer. It's her favorite," Adam said. He turned and looked at the guys. "We live two houses over, the green one to the left. We have plenty of room if you guys want to come over and let these two talk," he offered.

Clark shrugged his shoulders like he didn't care one way or the other. Levi nodded in agreement. And Jasper, he had a smartassed grin on his face. I knew by the look he had that what was about to come out of his mouth was going to piss me off.

"That's a stellar idea. As soon as these two love birds make up, we'll need earplugs. Trust and believe that. Please tell me you have some Jack over at your place or at least beer? It was a long-ass drive. And lover boy here," Jasper stopped and pointed at me, "was in such a hurry he wouldn't let us stop to pick some up. Even though I told him I needed beer to go with my chips. I figured we were in for a show, might as well have some refreshments."

Fucking Jasper, always had to be a wiseass. I don't think he knew how to take anything seriously. The woman I loved hated my guts, I made that happen, and his dumb ass wanted me to stop so he could get snacks like he was going to the movies. Jackass!

Adam and Anthony both laughed. "You're in luck, friend, I'm a bartender, and we have a fully stocked bar. We also have three guest rooms. Though I'm not sure which one of you is gonna fit in the twin sized bed we have in the smallest room, but I do know it's gonna be funny as hell to watch," Anthony said.

"I knew there was a reason I loved Lily. Of course she would have a bartender for a friend." Jasper slapped Levi on the back. "You ready for a little rematch?"

"We're not playing Go Fish ever again. You fucking cheat," Levi said.

"It's not my fault I have a damn near photographic memory," Jasper told him.

I can't believe these two idiots were standing in Lily's kitchen talking about Go Fish and I was still standing there listening to them argue when Lily was so close I could smell her flowery perfume. God, I missed her smell. I needed to find her.

"You two are morons. And Jasper, your memory sucks. You cheat. Now, get the hell outta here. I want to talk to Lily."

"Good luck," Adam said as he picked up a platter of watermelon.

"Man, I haven't played Go Fish since grade school. I'll play the winner." Anthony grabbed the plate with the burgers and started for the front door.

Jesus. I was surrounded by a bunch of adolescents. Clark waited for everyone to leave the room before coming close. "She loves you, Shane. No matter what she says to you, you have to remember that. She's gonna fight you. She has to, to save face. You not only broke her heart but hurt her pride as well. Good luck."

I scrubbed my hands over my face. He was right; I was in for the battle of my life, but I was ready. "Copy that."

Clark left me standing in the kitchen gathering my thoughts when it hit me. Clark had never, not once, called me Shane. I knew without a doubt that

Lily loved Shane, but I wasn't a hundred percent confident that she loved Lenox. I had to formulate a plan and a good one. When I discussed how I was going to win Lily back with the guys, I told them I was going to appeal to her sensible side. All three of them had laughed and told me good old-fashioned begging and pleading would work better. I didn't care what I had to do to get her back. The only thing I knew for certain was I was not leaving here without Lily and my baby. Lily was the most important thing in my life. She was my first love, my only love. Lily was my salvation, the baby was simply an added reward. I wanted them both, but I needed Lily to know that I loved her - baby or no baby.

I made my way down the hall and found a closed door at the end. I didn't bother knocking, it didn't matter if she answered the door or not; either way, I was going in. When I entered my gut twisted and guilt washed over me. Lily was lying on the bed curled in a ball. Even from the door, I could hear her soft sobs. Fuck. I am a complete dick.

I didn't bother saying a word as I climbed into the bed behind her, pulling her to me and wrapping my arms around her. My hands going to her pregnant belly, I closed my eyes and savored the feel of her. It was surreal knowing she was growing and nurturing our child. There were no words for what I felt at that moment, it only strengthened my resolve to win Lily back. I needed her more than anything in this world. My life would be meaningless without her.

"Are we gonna talk about the baby?" She broke the silence.

"No," I answered her. We had other things to discuss first.

"Don't you think we should talk about this? I understand if..."

It infuriated me she was about to suggest that I was the type of man who would or could walk away from her and my child, even if I had given her every reason to doubt me.

"Do not finish that statement, Lily. We'll talk about the baby later. There are more important things that we need to discuss first," I informed her. Lily tried to pull away from me, and my grip tightened carefully, making sure not to put too much pressure on her stomach. "Don't move."

"Let me go. I want to sit up."

"Oh no. We need to talk, and I haven't touched you for over five months."

"And whose fault is that?" Her body stiffened, but she stopped struggling.

I was hoping for a few more minutes to think about what I was going to say to her and just enjoy the feel of her.

"It's mine. All of this is my fault. There is so much I am sorry for. But, the first thing you gotta know is everything you said about me in Big Bear was the truth. I was being a coward and a liar. It was fucked up, and I will never stop being sorry for that. I thought that if I made you hate me, it would be easier for you to move on without me. You could be happy and live a normal life. I thought I had this stupid plan all worked out, but I forgot one important thing: you are the other half of my soul. You own me. I've spent every minute I was away from you missing you, going all the way back to the moment I left for basic. I've tried to be the better person and let you go. I can't do it anymore. I wasted so many years pushing my feelings for you aside, and I don't know if I can ever make up for that. But if you give me a chance, I swear to you I will spend every day of the rest of my life trying. You're my best friend."

"I can't," she whispered.

"Tell me what to do so you can," I pleaded.

"There's nothing you can do."

She began to shake in my arms, and I gently turned her. I needed to see her face. Tears leaked from the corners of her tightly closed eyes. "Look at me, sweetheart."

"Please just go." Lily kept her eyes closed and tried to hide her face.

I didn't know how to do this; the Army didn't teach me how to plead and beg for my girl's forgiveness. I was messing this up, and if I didn't figure out a way to fix it, I was going to lose her forever.

"I'm not going anywhere. I love you, and my life doesn't work without you."

"Don't say that. Do you know how hard this is for me? I have spent years trying to get over your death. Then you magically pop back to life, and I forgave you for that betrayal. But I can't forgive you for leaving me a second time. For months and months I've tried to stop loving you and move on with my life. And now you barge back into my life after you told me I'd never see you again and I'll have to start all over again. It's not just me anymore. I have to worry about what's right for the baby."

There was hope. She'd given me the in I needed. She said *tried to stop loving me*, not that she had stopped. Relief washed over me.

"Please, look at me." She was so damn stubborn that when she finally opened her eyes, she tried to look at anything and everything except me. However, I was a patient man - I'd wait forever if I had to. She must've run out of stuff to look at because she finally brought her shiny brown eyes to me and they were full of hurt. I did that to her. "I'm a fool. I'm trying to make this right. I'm going to fight for us, please stay and fight with me. I know I hurt you, I know I screwed up. But Lily, we are gonna move past this - there is no other option. Let's not forget you fucked up as well. When I tried to talk to you after we found you, you spouted off and lied too, pushing me away. And there is the baby. You walked away from me knowing that you were pregnant. And planned on keeping my child away from me."

"I did that for you," she said.

"For me? What the fuck? How is taking my kid and running for me?" I had to keep my mouth in check. As pissed off as I was about the baby, after talking with Jasper I could understand why she did what she did. As irrational and wrong as I thought it was, I got it. Getting mad about it now and losing my temper would do me no good. I had to let it go.

"You ripped my heart out," she cried. "I kept the baby a secret so you could live your life and not have to worry about us. I wasn't going to trap you. I knew you'd stay with me if you knew I was pregnant. I don't want to be an obligation, I won't let you leave the 707. You'll end up hating me and resenting the baby."

"I know I did." I took her face in my hands, making sure I had her full attention. "I was scared. I know now I can be good for you and still be good at my job. I could never hate you. Even if I left the 707 - you are worth it. Our family is more important to me than any job." I didn't wait for her to respond or tell me that I couldn't fix what I'd broken. I brought my lips to hers and took her mouth. She tasted like my past, my present, my home. I devoured her and poured every ounce of love I had into that kiss. I had to make her remember. "I need you to forget everything else and feel."

She moaned into my mouth and brought her hands to my tee, twisting it and pulling me closer. Her protruding belly preventing me from getting as close as I'd like.

"I love you, Lily." My hands wandered over her body, even with my eyes closed I knew every curve, every inch, every secret spot - it was all mine. "I'm gonna make you remember, I will make it impossible for you to leave me."

Something nudged my stomach, and I pulled back. "What was that?" I asked.

Lily's face lit up, and her eyes sparked to life. "The baby kicked."

"Holy shit, really?" I slid down her body and pulled her shirt up as I went, exposing her smooth, soft skin. I had never touched a bare pregnant belly before. Her stomach was tight and a perfect round shape. "Hi, baby," I whispered.

This time I saw it rather than felt it. My heart exploded with a love I'd never felt before. It was a different love than what I felt for Lily. Not more, not better, just different. A love a parent has for their child, unconditional and everlasting.

"Thank you," I choked out, so overcome with emotion I didn't care that tears had formed in my eyes. I wanted Lily to see how grateful I was for the gift she had given me.

Reality hit. I was going to be a father. Lily and I had created a life, a family.

23

He was here!

His lips were on my belly, and he was talking to the baby. I had spent so many nights crying and wishing that he was around to share this with me. Every time I felt the baby kick and move I questioned my every decision and my motives behind them. I was racked with guilt. I knew it was wrong to keep the baby from him and to deprive my child the love of his father, but I didn't know what else to do. I only wanted him to be happy.

Now here we were. My life, my happiness, and that of my child hung in the balance. We had both made so many mistakes and said hurtful things I was worried there was no coming back from that. But what the hell did I know about relationships? I wasn't raised in a happy home with loving parents who taught me what it meant to be partners with someone. My father was a selfish philanderer who only thought of himself and money. I never felt loved or cared for. The only person in my life who ever gave that to me was Shane, even though it was in a completely platonic and innocent way. It was easy and natural with us. We've always loved each other.

"I love you so much, I was willing to walk away and lose you if that meant you would be happy. I don't want you to give up anything to be with me. I was too afraid you'd end up detesting me for all the sacrifices you'd have to make," I admitted.

"As long as you are by my side I can never lose. You are my heart and my home. This baby doesn't trap me, he is our happily ever after. Don't take that from us, Lily. I know your intentions were good, but you made the wrong choice. We both did. Let's fix this and move on," he pleaded.

He was right; we were both at fault. Maybe the scales were balanced, each of our mistakes weighed just as heavy as the other's. I let his words soak in and remembered my life before he came back - it was sad and lonely. Then I tried to imagine my future without him by my side. It was the same dark, lonely place. Shane was not wrong, there was no other option. He was it for me, too. There was no one else in this world I would rather spend my life with. But knowing that still didn't mean I knew how to move past the mistakes.

"I'm sorry I lied and kept the baby from you. Can you forgive me?" I asked.

"Already forgotten. No looking back, we are going forward."

When his head lifted off my belly and his face came into clear view, only love and joy shined back.

"I missed you so much," I cried. The weight of the moment bore down on me. I could've lost him forever. Jasper was right, a thousand lifetimes wouldn't be enough to get over him.

Shane pulled himself up my body and kissed the tears off my cheeks. "Don't cry. No more tears, no more sadness. Only happiness from here on out. Me, you, and Carter."

The mention of our son's name only made the tears flow faster. I could've ruined that, too. All because of bad choices and fear.

"No more, sweetheart," he repeated.

His kiss started off as a slow burn starting in my belly and spreading outward in every direction. I desperately wanted to rip his clothes off and feel his bare skin. I'd read about hormones making women insatiable during the last part of pregnancy, but I had yet to experience them until now. The desire was overwhelming. I couldn't get him as close as I needed, couldn't soak up the taste of him fast enough. I wanted us connected in every way.

His hands went to my tender breasts. He found my nipples through my shirt, slowly circling them and making the throbbing in my pussy intensify. I'd had enough, I needed him now.

I reached down to pull my shirt off when my hand grazed my belly, reminding me my body was not what it used to be. I was hugely pregnant. What if Shane thought I looked gross or he was totally turned off by the change in my appearance? I had stretch marks forming on my hips, and I could barely shave my own legs now, let alone my lady bits. Damn, when was the last time I did that?

"What are you thinking about?" Shane asked, breaking the kiss.

"Nothing," I lied.

"Don't lie to me. You went from trying to climb inside of me to stiff as a board. Did I do something wrong, hurt the baby?" Shane pulled back.

"No, you didn't do anything wrong. The baby is fine." I buried my face in his neck and inhaled, loving his unique scent. "This is so embarrassing."

"You never have to be embarrassed with me, sweetheart."

"I'm pregnant," I announced.

"Yes, I can see that you are," Shane chuckled, his handsome face breaking out in a wide heart-stopping smile. He looked so happy, and I only felt worse for depriving him the knowledge of his son.

"I...um...look different," I stated the obvious.

"You do. And it's fucking hot."

"What? I'm huge, and I have stretch marks," I screeched. Was he crazy?

Shane rolled up on his elbow forcing me flat on my back. He silently looked down at me, and with wandering eyes, he scanned my entire body. Before I had time to protest Shane was on his knees and straddling my hips. My big belly front and center. His hands went to the hem of my shirt, and he pulled it up and off, leaving me in my bra.

"You are the sexiest woman I have ever seen. This right here," he placed both hands on my belly and began rubbing with a tenderness I'd never known, "makes me want to pound my chest like a caveman. Knowing that my son is growing inside of you makes me want to simultaneously wrap you up in cotton so nothing can hurt you and fuck the hell out of you."

I remained silent as his hands wandered down to the bottom of my belly to my hips, and he gently traced the new marks there.

"And these are proof of our love. Every new stripe you earn while our child is growing will be worth it. These will remind us that we can overcome anything. They are not any old scars, sweetheart, they are the marks of a woman. My woman who has carried, nurtured, and kept my son safe. Every damn part of you is sexy."

Damn, I loved this man. I felt every word he said deep in my heart.

"I love you," I whispered.

"Enough to come home with me and marry me?" Shane asked.

"Yes."

"I want a big family, Lily. I want to fill our house up with as many kids as we can. I want to make the home that we never had," Shane told me.

"Okay." I didn't trust my voice to say any more than that.

"I'm going to make love to you now." This time Shane didn't wait for my reply before he pulled my shorts and panties down my legs and tossed them away. "Roll on your side, I want you from behind so I can hold you close."

I took off my bra and did what he asked. Shane stood and pulled his shirt over his head and when he bent to pull his boots off something on his back caught my attention.

"What's that?" I asked.

"What's what?" he asked as his boot thudded on the wood floor, and he looked up at me still bent.

"On your back. Did you get another tattoo?"

Shane's face blushed pink, only piquing my interest more. I don't think I'd ever seen Shane blush.

"Yes," he answered and stood to his full height, undoing his belt and allowing his pants to fall around his ankles.

He was so damn hot my mouth watered. All thoughts of tattoos, and stretch marks, and big bellies flew from my head. The only thought left was that I wanted him inside of me, and now.

He turned to check that my bedroom door was locked, giving me a clear, unobstructed view of his tight ass. My eyes walked further up, and I froze.

"Oh my God," I choked out.

"After you left, I missed you so much. I was reckless and dangerous to my team. I was completely lost without you. I needed something. I had to have a piece of us. That's when I got it. I no longer had your charm, but now a permanent reminder of you and our shared past," he explained.

The tattoo was spectacular, but the artwork wasn't the most beautiful thing about it. It was the meaning behind it. It was almost an exact replica of my Tree of Life pendant.

"It's perfect. I can't believe you remembered what it looked like."

"The moment I placed that necklace around your neck and the pendant fell in between your tits is forever burned into my memory. You looked so pretty that day on the boardwalk. I almost broke down and professed my love for you. Damn, I wish I would've done it. I swear, that day I was ready to ask you to run away with me."

"We were teenagers," I reminded him.

"I knew then that you were the girl I wanted to spend my life with. I'm so fucking sorry I wasted so much time. I'm sorry I wasn't strong enough. I promise you, Lily, that not a moment will go by I won't make sure you know how much I love you. I swear I will make you happy."

"You already do. All of that is in the past, remember? No more looking back. We have a future to plan and a present to live."

Shane crawled into bed and pulled me close.

The heat of his bare chest on my back made me squirm with excitement.

"I love feeling that ass grind against my cock, but I need you to hold still," he scolded.

"Holy shit. Shane!" I groaned as he pushed his full length inside of me.

"So. Damn. Good," he paused in between each word, "to be home." I wiggled my ass some more trying to get him to go faster. "Stay still, Lily," he warned. "This is gonna be slow and sweet. I want to make love to my girl."

And he did. It was slow and deliciously torturous. He brought us both off and started all over again. By the time he was done, I was a boneless, sated, happy woman.

"Are you ready for banana ice cream yet?" he asked when we were finished and cleaned up.

"What?" I laughed.

"Adam told me it was your favorite. Would you like some?" he explained.

Ice cream had been the last thing on my mind the last few hours, but now that he brought it up it did sound good.

"Yes, please," I said.

"I'll get you a bowl." Shane knifed out of bed, uncaring that he was naked. Why would he? His body was magnificent. A renaissance artist couldn't have sculpted a better physique.

"Just bring the whole pint," I called out when he opened the bedroom door.

I stared at my ceiling listening to his laughter as he walked down the hall. The sound filled my soul. Shane was back. In the span of a few hours, my life had once again changed drastically. Only this time I wasn't going to run. I wasn't going to let untruths and misguided choices screw me out of happiness. I was taking it and holding on with both hands. Shane was right; he was my happily ever after.

THAT NIGHT SHANE and I stayed up until the wee hours of the morning just like old times. We talked about everything and nothing. I didn't care what words were actually spoken as long as I was wrapped in his arms.

"The sun is almost up. Let's go out to the shore," Shane suggested.

"I'd love that."

He helped me get dressed, making sure I bundled up so I'd stay warm. We grabbed a blanket off the porch and headed down to the water. When we sat, he threaded his fingers through mine and brought them up to his mouth, kissing each digit.

"Thank you," he said breaking the silence.

"For?" I asked.

"For the second chance. For my son. For making me so happy. For agreeing to be my wife. The list is long. I think it'll take the rest of my life to tell you everything I am thankful for."

"Lucky for you we have a lifetime."

Sitting on the shore, we made plans for our future. The future we'd almost lost. A future that was sure to be as bright and beautiful as the morning sunrise before us.

The reds gave way to orange, and the orange changed into brilliant yellow. As the sun made its way over the horizon, Shane held me close whispering how much he loved me and the baby.

All too soon I heard male voices behind us.

"'Bout time you two came out of the love shack," Jasper yelled.

I couldn't help but laugh at him.

"Idiot," Shane mumbled under his breath.

"You two ready to get on the road?" Clark asked.

Shane and I answered at the same time.

"Yes."

"No."

"No?" Shane asked.

"I need to talk to Adam and Anthony. And I have to say goodbye to Miss Milly. Plus, I have to pack my stuff."

"No need." I heard and turned to look at Adam as he joined us on the shoreline. "Take what you need, and stop to say goodbye to Gran on your way out of town. She'll be pleased as pie you're leaving. Anthony and I will bring the rest of your stuff when we come down next week," he explained.

"Come down? You'll visit in Georgia?" I asked.

"You aren't getting rid of us so easily. Besides, now that you have your man back and the travel ban to Georgia has been lifted, we were hoping you'd do the design work on the new remodel. We'll drop your stuff and the plans off to you."

"Yes," I answered and threw my arms around Adam. "Thank you. I can't tell you how much your friendship means to me," I whispered.

"We love you, Lily. I'm so happy for you," he whispered back.

"All of what Adam said," Anthony started. "And Mr. Eye Candy over there is a Go Fish cheater. I am demanding a rematch," Anthony continued, pointing at Jasper.

"Mr. Eye Candy? That is fucking unbelievably

funny. I think Jasper has a new call sign," Shane laughed beside me.

"I don't fucking cheat, I just have a good memory. Ya'll are a bunch of sore losers. And, hey, I can't help how supremely sexy I am." Jasper winked.

"Supremely sexy? Who are you? Zoolander, the male model?" Levi asked.

"Jealous much?" Jasper shot back.

My smile was so wide, my cheeks started to hurt. I couldn't remember a time when I was so happy and my future was so bright.

"Idiot," Shane grumbled still smiling. He might like to call Jasper an idiot and pretend he was annoyed, but he didn't fool me. He loved these guys.

"Come on, Bluesteel. Help Lily pack. We have a mission brief in six hours," Clark barked as he started back toward the house.

Shit. A mission, that meant Shane was leaving.

"I don't have to go. I can put in for leave." Shane stopped in front of me.

"Yes, you do. You have a job to do, and I have a house to get ready for the baby," I replied.

"I'll be safe. I promise I'll come home to you," he whispered.

"And I promise I will be there waiting."

The End

To read the extended epilogue please download your **free** copy here.

https://dl.bookfunnel.com/r7xz1y4reo

Continue reading for a sneak peak of Freeing Jasper Book 2 – Jasper and Emily's story.

FREEING JASPER

PROLOGUE

Jasper

"Yo! Anyone home?" I walked in the front door without knocking.

"You know Lenox is gonna give you shit for just walking in his house," Levi said laughing as I opened the door and let myself in.

"That's what makes it so fun." What could I say? Riling Lenox up was amusing.

"I'm in the kitchen," Lily yelled.

Levi and I made our way to the kitchen, and my stomach growled. Lily had a metric shit ton of food spread out over the counter. God, I loved that woman. Maybe I'd consider not annoying Lenox today, in appreciation for him bringing us Lily.

"Hey, Lily," Levi said and pulled her in for a hug.

"Thanks for having us over, everything looks great," I noted.

After Lily came to Georgia and moved in with Lenox, and especially after Carter was born, the team had taken to backyard barbeques and poker at their house. It was a far cry from our nights together bar hopping after we got home from a mission. I was happy for Lenox, him and Lily both. After all their years apart, they deserved to be happy.

"One of these days I'm gonna beat your ass for walking into my house without knocking. And keep your voices down, I just put Carter to sleep," Lenox commented when he came in the room.

"Doubtful," I shot back.

"Doubtful I'll do it? Or doubtful I can? Because I think I proved not too long ago I can put you on your ass."

He wished.

"Man, you sucker punched me. It doesn't count," I said, picking up a cracker and shoving it in my mouth.

"You're so full of shit. I warned you I was gonna kick your ass. It wasn't my fault you didn't believe me."

He did. He warned me the night I told him that Lily was pregnant and I had kept it from him. I didn't regret keeping Lily's secret, I would do it again. They needed time to get their shit together and heal from everything that had happened. They had both said things to each other they didn't mean. I knew a little bit about saying things that you could never take back – I didn't want my friend to suffer the same fate I had.

In an effort to push Lily away, in some misguided effort to protect her, Lenox had said some pretty brutal stuff to her. Including lying to her, telling her he had never loved her. When the truth was, he had loved her his whole life. It was all for naught when Lily was kidnapped and held in the Bahamas by a madman. After we rescued Lily, she knew she was pregnant, but hadn't told anyone. I made the decision to not tell Lenox. Lily had already made up her mind she was going to run. There was nothing that Lenox could've said to make her stay. It would've only further driven a wedge between them. I let Lily leave without telling Lenox. They both needed time. When her time ran out, the team and I took Lenox to her. In the end, it was the right choice. Lenox and Lily were happily married with a son they both adored.

Only, Lenox didn't actually give me a beat down or kick my ass, he sucker punched me in the face, and I didn't hit him back. That's how men worked their shit out. It was easy; a man gets pissed, he punches another man in the face, we move on. It was so much easier than what women did – bitch and drag it on, forever rehashing it every chance they got.

"No more talking about the fight. We're here to eat, drink, and play poker," Lily chastised.

"But Lily, this is what real men do. We talk about fighting, fucking, and killing bad guys," Levi helpfully explained.

The look of shock on Lily's face was hysterical. I knew she thought that Levi was the most mild-mannered out of the group because he rarely cursed in front of her. Boy was she wrong. We all had our own special skillset when we were in the field. Each of us brought something unique that made our team the best there was. Levi was ice-cold when we were on a mission. Not even I could turn off my emotions the way he could, and he was brutal when he needed to be. And the cursing? He had Lily snowed; that man came up with some pretty creative words for tangos.

"Seriously?" Lily asked.

I had to laugh when Lily turned to Lenox for help.

"Well, sweetheart, he's not wrong," Lenox confirmed.

I thought I heard Lily mumble *men* under her breath, but there was a knock at the door before I could comment.

"For tonight, while I have a friend over, can we please limit the talk about fighting, fucking, and killing?"

"We'll see what we can do," Shane replied, smiling at his wife.

"Is she hot?" I couldn't help asking. I didn't bother hiding my enjoyment of women around my team. I know they probably thought I got laid more than I actually did, I just didn't bother correcting them.

"Not answering that," Lily shouted back as she went for the door.

"Dude, what happened to the blonde from last night?" Levi asked.

Yes, the blonde. She was sexy as hell and fake. Every part of her from her glued-on lashes to the porno-style moans. Boring. A dime a dozen. We both had fun and parted ways. No hard feelings.

"Do you want details or the cliff notes?" I joked.

"Not even worth the normal week?" Lenox laughed.

"She kicked me outta her bed with a thanks-for-coming-don't-call-again. I smiled and left," I explained.

Levi or Lenox said something, but I'd lost interest when I heard the sweetest voice come from the other room. I couldn't make out the words, something about whiskey maybe. It was the tone of her voice, the cadence. The kind of voice that would soothe and lull you to sleep. Just the sound of it alone hit me in the gut. She wouldn't fake her moans, she would enjoy her man, actually *feel* him.

"Come in. The guys are in the kitchen, and if you want to eat, we'd better hurry," I heard Lily say.

Holy fuck.

In walked the prettiest woman I had ever seen. Long midnight hair that was made to have a man wrap around his hand. Crystal blue eyes made even more beautiful by her skin tone, not makeup. I didn't even think the girl was wearing any. Her beauty was all her – all real, no pretense, nothing fake.

"Hi, Emily. Nice to see you again, thanks for coming over," Lenox said.

His voice pulled me from my stupor, reminding me I was in front of my team.

"Hey, Lenox. Thanks for having me," the woman, Emily, replied.

"This is Jasper and Levi, Shane's teammates." Lily pointed at each of us.

"Hi. I'm Emily." Her sweet voice was even better close up.

"Nice to meet you," Levi politely said.

"Yo," I greeted. When her eyes came to me, I could've sworn I saw a flash of interest. I had to know for sure so I added a wink.

Emily blushed. Hell yeah!

"You from around here, Emily?" I asked for no other reason than I wanted to hear her voice.

Before Emily could answer, there was a honk from out front that drew everyone's attention away.

"That must be Clark," Lenox said.

Shit, I forgot. Another reason we were here today. We were going to build Carter a swing set. I followed Lenox and Levi to the front door without getting to hear Emily's answer.

The door shut behind us and Lenox turned to me. "Lily will have your balls if you fuck with Emily, brother. And while I'm not fond of that visual, better she removes yours than mine."

"Fuck with her? I don't want to fuck with her," I told him.

"You didn't exactly hide the fact you were eye fucking her," Levi added.

"I was not eye fucking her. If I was, she would've been panting. I won't lie, she's fucking gorgeous."

"But? There's normally a *but* after the phrase, *I won't lie*," Levi asked.

"No buts. Just acknowledging the fact, she's beautiful."

Lenox stared at me, something weird working behind his eyes. "What?" I prompted.

"Huh. I'm not used to you calling women beautiful or gorgeous. Sexy and hot are your normal adjectives."

"You're way overthinking this. Let's get this lumber in the backyard so we can eat," I said.

Damn, nothing gets past that fucker. The truth was she was both hot and sexy, but it seemed beneath her to describe her that way. She wasn't some barfly I wanted to take home for the night. Not that I wouldn't mind some alone time with her. But more than that, I wanted to talk to her, take her to dinner so I could hear her laugh. I bet she had a great laugh.

Continue reading Freeing Jasper - getbook.at/freeingjasper

NIGHTSTALKER

Zane

Fuck! I let out an exaggerated sigh when I saw the caller information on my phone. I glanced at the old-fashioned grandfather clock that sat in the corner of my office noting it was well past stopping time. Closing the lid to my laptop I walked over to the floor to ceiling windows in my office admiring the Naval Academy at night. The Yard was lit up and looked like a city unto itself, the Chapel Dome standing tall and proud above the rest of the buildings. The still ringing phone in my hand pulled me from my reverie.

Entering my ten-digit security code I swiped the

screen to take the call. Before my phone was even to my ear I could hear the caller's impatient voice.

"It's time," the voice over the phone sounded tired and far away.

"Fuck me. Now?" I closed my eyes praying for patience.

"Zane, man, I have waited long enough. I am done."

"I know you have, I am afraid I will lose her once she knows the truth."

"It's time," he repeated.

"Brace brother, she is not the same woman she was." I have tried to warn him hundreds of times.

"Fuck you. You don't think I know who she is?" He shot back, his temper rising.

"Don't say I didn't warn you when you are one nut short of a pair." I smiled at the thought.

"Copy that, see you soon."

The line went dead, and I pocketed my phone as I continued to stare out the window. I was going to enjoy what was left of my peace. A shit storm was about to invade my perfectly ordered world. Now I had one more call to make before I could call it a night. Checking the clock again, I entered my ten-digit security code and dialed the secured number I knew from memory. The clicking sound before the call connected alerted me that the call was indeed encrypted.

"Password of the day?" a gruff sounding man asked.

"Zulu, Charlie, Foxtrot, Niner," I replied.

"Certified. Hold for connection," the monotone voice put my call through.

"Zane, How are you this evening? Working late I see." I could hear the chuckle in his voice.

"Yes, Sir. I have an update for you Mr. President; he is on his way stateside," I advised the President.

"Took that son of a bitch long enough! I am surprised he waited this long. Thanks for the update. And Zane, one more thing - how many times do I have to tell you to call me Tom when we are having a conversation amongst friends?" The President sounded almost giddy. I, for one, did not understand what there was to be happy about.

"Yes, Tom. Sorry to have bothered you so late. I will keep you apprised of the situation." Even saying the name "Tom" while talking to the, President of the United States had me looking over my shoulder waiting for a court martial.

"We'll be in touch." I could hear his peal of laughter as the line went dead.

Jasmin

Whizzz, snap! That was the last sound the poor asshole lying on the nasty assed, stained carpet in front of me heard, as my 147 grain subsonic bullet lodged in his brain. Before his blood even had a chance to pool around his head I had already unscrewed the suppressor off my Sig Sauer P226, affectionately known as Penelope, and carefully holstered her. Yes, I named my weapons, and she was beautiful. Right down to her custom grip, designed to fit my small hands, and her dark earth finish. Penelope was the love of my life.

I know. You don't have to say it. For a twenty-eight-year-old woman, that is pretty fucking sad.

I looked around the room at my team, noting the half empty bottles of beer and endless bags of takeout strewn about. The unfortunate bastard's body had barely hit the floor, and they were already at work gathering the electronic devices that blanketed every available surface of his makeshift work station. I watched as they meticulously placed each laptop, external hard drives, and computer towers into shock resistant transport cases. Any piece of electronic equipment that could store information would be coming with us today. This included the 1990's era CD player.

Christ, this asshole was a slob. His apartment smelled like he hadn't cleaned a toilet in a year. The strong odor of urine permeated the small living room. There was a month's worth of energy drinks and coffee to-go cups littering every available dirty surface. The trash can was overflowing with God knows what.

"Jesus, anyone else need a biohazard mask?" Jaxon noted the vile smell of the room as he pushed aside a to-go cup full of cigarette butts. You wouldn't think a little piss and cigarette smoke smell would bother a former USAF Special Forces Pararescueman.

"For someone who sold information for ten grand a pop, he sure lived in a hellhole," Eric added, looking at the stained, 1960's era plaid couch.

"Fuck, man, he must have invested all of his money into machines. Garrett is going to go ape shit over this equipment. I hope Z has found another specialist to help him analyze all of this. He is already three cases deep," Drew replied as he gently placed a tower into a case, the two inch foam giving way under the weight of the heavy machine.

"Yeah, this guy hasn't been laid in years. He has two air conditioner units on full blast in his bedroom and a dirty mattress just lying on the floor. It looks like a server room met hoarders in there. I need another case for all the drives in that room alone." Leo waved a hand in front of his face as he walked back into the main room, presumably to get the piss smell to dissipate.

I stood over the dead guy and watched the blood ooze out of the bullet wound, down the bridge of his nose, and over his cheek. Finally it joined a growing puddle of thick red liquid on the filthy, stained carpet next to his ear.

It was a damn clean shot. One and done.

"Yo, Jasmin you thinkin' about helping here, or you gonna just keep staring at the stiff?" Colin spoke from across the room where he was gathering up flash drives.

"Just admiring my shot placement, Cap. I swear I get better every time." I flashed my best, "I'm the shit" smile and looked over Louis Clark, better known as *Deepweb336* to the slimy underbelly of the deep web one last time, "Perfectly placed, right between the eyes. The bastard ought to thank me." I made over to help the guys finish up.

The bastard lay dead in the middle of his living room. He barely had the chance to react before I made my way into his apartment, and took my shot. The two deadbolts on his door were a joke; it took me all of five seconds to pick each lock. For a world class hacker he was pretty lax on his personal security. Single cylinder deadbolts were child's play.

"Ya'll are a bunch of pansy asses complaining about the smell. If I didn't know any better I'd swear you were all trained by the girl scouts." I loved to tease the guys when I could. It was a rare occasion they acted like a bunch of sissies complaining about smell and filth.

"Fuck me, Jas thinks she has jokes. Who do you think contracted the douche to hack into the spooks database?" Eric asked with a look of disdain on his face. The CIA had burned him on his last assignment. They fucked him over so badly that even years later he still refused to even be in the same room with an agent. "My guess is the Russians."

"Eric your guess is always the Russians," Colin threw in as he latched another container and placed it on a dolly.

Deepweb336 had been on radar for years. He was a low-level hacker when we first caught up with him. He slowly made a name for himself stealing corporate secrets and selling them to any competitor that was willing to add a bunch of zeros to whatever number he threw out.

Z Corps, and the government agencies that ran contracts through us, never gave two shits what Deepweb336 did, only that he was quickly making a name for himself as one of the most sought after hackers in the world. That is, until he tried to hack into the CIA database that held information on where undercover agents were on assignment. Stealing that would have led to an outrageous number of casualties, pissed off most foreign governments, and made the people in power have to answer some very uncomfortable questions.

Deepweb336 needed to be eliminated before those questions were asked. Z Corps took the contract to do just that. That and to recover any information he might have already stolen. Red Team was the best recovery team the company had ever trained; the team that got sent out on the highest priority ops. And this op was high priority. It was top secret shit that was so far above my paygrade I didn't know all the players involved and never would unless Zane, my boss, felt that information was required for me to do my job. Z Corps recruited and contracted some of the world's best hackers and deep web information brokers; it would be their job to sift through all the machines we brought back. It would also be their job to find out who had hired Deepweb336. It's a shame he turned out to be such a douche and played for the wrong team his skills could have been an asset to Z Corps.

"We need to be out in six minutes. Cargo will be out front." Colin, the team leader, yelled, reminding us of our deadline.

"Aye aye Cap." The team echoed in unison.

We were six minutes until, out the door, all electronics needed to be packed up and ready for transport. The last of the hacker's equipment was dismantled and placed into plastic containers. The rest of the team speedily donned mover's coveralls created for today's transport. Today they were "Movers on the Go". MoGo. A cargo van would be waiting for them at the entrance with a MoGo logo on the side.

Colin and I stayed in the everyday clothes we wore in, nothing too flashy that would make us stand out. This was a shit neighborhood after all; we needed to blend in like we belonged in this rat-infested apartment complex. We would not be going out with the "movers" today we would act as their back up.

"We're out. See ya back at HQ," Drew said as he pulled his hat lower on his head in an effort to shield his face, a habit we all had. The team had already done a sweep of the apartment complex checking for any video surveillance inside of the building. It was no surprise that the old, shithole complex had no such devices. That only left the traffic cameras to be disabled en route. The guys back at HQ would handle that. Eric, Jaxon, and Leo followed Drew out the door. Each had a dolly stacked high with black plastic hard cases.

Colin grabbed my hand once we were in the hallway, and walked us hand in hand out of the building. Once we were on the street we could watch the team as they loaded the cargo van. With a quick sweep of the street Colin kissed my forehead and walked us across the intersection like an everyday couple.

Pulling my secure, encrypted cellphone out of my pocket, careful not to advertise the pistol strapped underneath my jacket, I punched in my ten-digit security code.

"Cleanup is a go." I ended the call and slid my phone back into my pocket. I looked up at Colin and smiled brightly. Another successful mission. The cleaners would be there soon and it would look like Louis Clark never lived there at all.

Continue reading here –
mybook.to/nightstalkerRT

ACKNOWLEDGMENTS

A special thanks to my two Alpha readers – Michelle Thomas and Chriss Prokic. Thank you both so much for all your help on this book.

Elfwerks Editing took my normal jumbled up mess and polished it. Thank you for all your hard work. Your notes and suggestion undoubtedly made this book better.

To the BETA readers, reviewers, and Bloggers that took time out of their lives to read, review and promote this project – THANK YOU! As with anything else in life it takes a village. I couldn't have published this book without your help.

Ellie Masters – Thank you. Your friendship, guidance, and steadfast support means the world to me. I wouldn't have finished this book when I did if it wasn't for your word sprints. You truly are one-of-a-kind.

Kendall Barnett – My business partner and friend -You are the bomb dot com. I love you woman!

ALSO BY RILEY EDWARDS

Riley Edwards

www.RileyEdwardsRomance.com

Romantic Suspense

Gemini Group

Nixon's Promise

Red Team

Nightstalker

Protecting Olivia - Susan Stoker Universe

Redeeming Violet - Susan Stoker Universe

Recovering Ivy - Susan Stoker Universe

Rescuing Erin - Susan Stoker Universe

Romancing Rayne - Susan Stoker Universe

The Gold Team

Brooks - Susan Stoker Universe

The 707 Freedom Series

Free

Freeing Jasper

Finally Free

Freedom

The Next Generation (707 spinoff)

Saving Meadow

Chasing Honor

Finding Mercy

Claiming Tuesday

Adoring Delaney

The Collective

Unbroken

Trust

ABOUT THE AUTHOR

Riley Edwards is a bestselling multi-genre author, wife, and military mom. Riley was born and raised in Los Angeles but now resides on the east coast with her fantastic husband and children.

Riley writes heart-stopping romance with sexy alpha heroes and even stronger heroines. Riley's favorite genres to write are romantic suspense and military romance.

Don't forget to sign up for Riley's newsletter and never miss another release, sale, or exclusive bonus material.

https://www.subscribepage.com/RRsignup

Facebook Fan Group

www.rileyedwardsromance.com